home, these

Skateboard tried to lure him down into it with
prom
tripp
VCR
mo'

He   *is a fucking set-up. Once the fire dies down, niggers
is gon' pay for this and I'm gon' be in Ghana, West
Africa.*

He stutter-stepped back into the living room.
The analysts were analyzing the analysts, the pundits were punditing, the sociologists were sociologizing, the urbanologists were making money, people were being interviewed.

A young black man with his Raiders cap on sideways summed it up: "If you have to ask me why
this happened 'cause you really don't know, then
my daddy was right, white folks is a bunch o'
dumb motherfuckers!"

MIDNIGHT

ODIE HAWKINS

An Original Holloway House Edition
HOLLOWAY HOUSE PUBLISHING COMPANY
LOS ANGELES, CALIFORNIA

Published by
HOLLOWAY HOUSE PUBLISHING COMPANY
8060 Melrose Avenue, Los Angeles, CA 90046

This is a work of fiction. Names, characters, places, and incidents
are either the product of the author's imagination or are used fic-
titiously. Any resemblance to actual events or locales or persons,
living or dead, is entirely coincidental.

International Standard Book Number 0-87067-738-1
Printed in the United States of America

Cover illustration by Richard Dunn, Allied Artists
Cover design by Paul M. Papp

MIDNIGHT

MIDNIGHT

1

Clyde Johnson, better known as "Bop Daddy" to the hundreds of gang bangers he used to lead and hang out with, stared at the scenes on the television fascinated.

Where's the police?

The television reporter circling Florence and Normandie in the channel 7 newscopter echoed Bop's thought question. "Where are the police? The police are nowhere to be seen. Motorists are being pulled from their vehicles by roving groups of young black men and beaten. A truck driver is sprawled on the ground next to his vehicle; he has been brutally beaten and stomped.

"Several other motorists driving through this intersection of Florence and Normandie in the heart of South Central Los Angeles have been assaulted by young blacks. There appears to be a racially motivated pattern to these attacks. This is Bob Murphy, reporting to you from the channel 7 newscopter. Now back to the studio. Joann, Fred?"

Bop flicked past channels 9 through 13 and back to channels 2, 5, and 9 and finally back to channel 7 again.

Where's the police?

"The police have not arrived on the scene as of yet, and it is a well-known fact that Chief Daryl Gates set aside a million-dollar overtime contingency fund for just such an emergency as this. Where are the police?"

Bop stood with his fists on his hips, mesmerized by the sight of the roving groups of mostly young black men and women, shifting from one side of the street to the other.

The liquor store on the northwest corner of the intersection was being looted. Bop backed away from the television, turned the corner to go into the kitchen for a Beck's beer.

Uhh ooohh..., them young niggers done got hold of that fire water now....

He propped himself up in his uncle David's chair, sipping his beer, alternating his urges.... *Damn, I bet Skateboard, Bone, Big Fool, and the rest of 'em are down there or they're trying to get down there. Wish I was there.*

He leaned forward to stare at the figures racing around on the wide screen. Color TV makes everything look like fun.

No police howwww! They could shut this shit down right now if they wanted to. Wonder why they're not putting the muscle on?

The Watts Riot was taking place, May, 1992; the earlier Watts "riot" had been revolt, this was clearly a riot happening. Bop leaned back in his chair, sipped his beer, and stared out of the sliding picture window to his left.

Torrance, 228th Street, California. The low stand of mint next to the cactus was a deep green (he had dried some and mixed it with his marijuana a few times), the figs were ripe, the tangerines and oranges were sweetening on the trees. It was a sunny day.

Six months ago I would've been right down there in the middle of all that craziness.

He sipped his beer and checked the wall clock. Uncle David and Aunt Lulu would be pulling in in a couple of hours, loaded with goodies. He looked around the living room for something to do.

There wasn't a helluva lot of housework to do with three neat adults on the premises (especially the way Aunt Lulu could take a broom, a mop, and a dishrag once a week), which gave Bop days of watching the soaps, the talk shows, and the news.

Sweet people, Uncle David and Aunt Lulu.

"Now let's get something straight right off the bat. I'm your uncle, you Marvina's boy, bless her soul, and I want to see that you have the best that you can have in this life. You twenty-one years already an' you ain't done shit with your life but fuck it up...."

"Dave, don't talk to the boy like that, he...."

"It's OK, Aunt Lulu, he's right. I need to hear this. Go 'head, Unc, tell it like it is."

Uncle David was famous for the "overkill speech."

"All right now, like I was sayin', you ain't done shit with your life so far but fuck it up. You was effing it up in Chicago when you was nine or ten and you ain't done a helluva lot better since your ass got out here."

Uncle David could get to the core of things faster than most people. Bop flashed on the image of himself..., "effing up" in Chicago, playing hooky, stealing, getting caught, worrying momma to death with all kinds of negative shit.

Yeahh, Unc, you're right.

"You got out here, where a nigger at least has a decent chance, and you kept on effing up. You wanted to box but you didn't want to train, so them li'l wetbacks wiped the ring up with your ass. You thought you wanted to be a big-time pimp-drug dealer, but the cops outsmarted you 'cause they got computers 'n shit.

"Now then, I'm gon' tell you something you may already know; the only game in town is money—M-O-N-E-Y—and if you don't have any, your own momma don't like you.

9

"Now then, there's only a few ways to get money. You can work for it, like me and your Aunt Lu. You can inher-it, which ain't nobody done in our family so far, or you can steal it.

"The best way is to work for it. You know why? If you sit around on your ass waitin' for somebody to die, they may not leave you shit anyway. And if you think you smart enough to get 'way with stealin' it, well, just take a look at the prisons. You've had your share of that, I hope.

"Betch' every one of those dudes thought they could get away with stealin', but they didn't, so now they doin' time.

"Much as I dislike to say it, the best way to get the money is to work for it. When you work for it, people can't accuse you for doin' nothing wrong."

Bop smiled at the memory of his Uncle's speech, of the memory of Aunt Lu's head tilted back on the sofa, glasses on the tip of her nose, sound asleep.

Where's the police? He gulped the last quarter of the beer and leaned forward to circle the channels again.

The South Central Los Angeles reaction to the Rodney King verdict (of not guilty for the four white cops accused of beating a black man senseless) was heating up.

Bop watched the flames shooting out of a car that had wandered into the riot zone.

Uhhhh ooohh, here we go..., the fire....

He strolled into the kitchen, opened the refrigerator door, and quickly pulled another Beck's from the box. He forced himself to ignore the pies, ham, packages of salami, left-over buckets of fried chicken, potato salad, half gallons of ice cream. He was trying to keep his weight down to 165.

"I work for my livin' 'n I like po'k chops. Don't we, Lu?"

"Always have."

They worked hard (a mailman and a grammar school teacher—"they know as much about sin in the fourth grade

10

as they'll ever know, these days"). They had offered him the opportunity to live with them for a few months, to "pull his act together."

"Now, Bop, you got to understand, we love you. You're the only nephew your uncle has out here in California and we want to see you make something out of yourself."

"I hope you're takin' Aunt Lulu to heart 'cause we're too old to be tryin' to track you down at night and make sure you're not usin' dope or sellin' dope or stealin' or runnin' around with the rest of them crazy fools in Watts. You either decide you're gonna pull it together here, go to school, get a job or whatever, or move on. You understand what I'm sayin' to you?"

"I read you loud 'n clear, Unc, loud 'n clear."

The telephone ringing jarred him, janged his hand on the beer bottle.

"Hello."

"Heyyy, Bop? That you?" Bone's heavy grained voice came at him.

"Who in the fuck you callin'?"

Bone cracked up; he was a freak for Bop's offbeat sense of humor. He gave him a few moments of laughter.

Sounds like he's clearing his fuckin' throat when he laughs.

"Well, c'mon, motherfucker, speak."

It took Bone a few more seconds of hacking, coughing, laughing before he could answer. "Mannn, you still outta your skull, you know that?!"

"Yeahh, I know, Bone, what's happenin'?"

"Uhhh, what about this shit goin' down, man; what we gon' do…?"

"Fuck, you mean, what we gon' do?"

"Well, you know what I mean, what the Bricks gon' do?"

"You called the wrong brother, home. I cut the Bricks

11

loose six months ago, remember?"

"Awww c'mon, Bop, let's cut the bullshit, man; you the top Brick!"

"Bone, listen to me close, man, listen to me close; I *was* the top Brick. Dig it? I *was*...."

He gently replaced the receiver in its wall cradle and stood in place, sipping his brew, feeling half an urge to call Bone back, one of the top level Bricks he had "made," and feeling half disgusted.

Why can't these motherfuckers think of nothing to do on their own: why does someone always have to be telling them what to do?

"Bop, couple thangs you got to understand. Most people are just milling around like sheep, waiting for someone to lead them somewhere. They're natural followers, most people."

"Awww c'mon, Chester, I don't believe that."

"If it wasn't true you wouldn't be doing time in here for leading a gang through South Central Los Angeles, inciting a riot."

"I was framed; I didn't do nothing."

"Sure you did, you led one hundred and fifty-three young brothers in a protest march from Century and Main to Imperial Bloulevard."

"Somebody had to do it, man."

"Why did it have to be you?"

* * * * *

The car pulled into the driveway; Uncle David and Aunt Lu were home. The riot was four hours old and had spread from Florence and Normandie to Manchester and Vermont. And points in between.

Uncle David and Aunt Lulu had a precision honed schedule; he left the Beverly Hills post office at 2:30 P.M., picked his wife up at the Progressive School on Pico and Overland Boulevard at 3:15 P.M., and—on the days when they didn't stop for fresh supplies of top-grade steaks, farm-raised catfish, steak-sized pork chops, top-of-the-line poultry, cake, pies, and other goodies—they were easing into the driveway by ten to four.

"Ain't too much a po' man can do 'cept eat good. I ain't never heard of a dollar bill that filled up a man's gut or stopped him from feeling thirsty."

Uncle David had an answer for most of the questions that the world seemed to want answers for.

"If you want to get somewhere or do something, the first thing you have to do is git up off your ass and move!"

Bop peeked out of the window, his third Beck's in hand, and smiled as he watched his uncle and aunt get out of the car.

They were massive people; Uncle David at six foot one, carried a 285 pound Sumo wrestler's belly in front of him. Aunt Lulu matched her man's bulk with her own five foot eight, two hundred well-packed pounds. She was, as the saying put it, full up front and ample behind.

And they had to lean back in the late model car, get their thick legs on the ground, and then edge out of the vehicle. He had seen both of them struggle to ease from behind the wheel at least three or four times. On one occasion he thought he'd have to help Aunt Lulu wedge free, but she made it without his help.

They were fifty-one and forty-nine (Aunt Lu sometimes fudged back to forty-six), solid, quiet-moving people who paid their dues, didn't take any guff from anybody, and were determined to live what they called "the good life."

"Everybody has to do what they think is right."

They worked, ate, watched television, and, on special

occasions, went out for a lobster dinner on the pier at Redondo Beach.

"What them young niggers doin' now?"

Uncle David wedged himself in front of Bop to stare at the helicopters whirling over the sections of Los Angeles that were being set on fire.

Aunt Lu headed straight for their bedroom to change into her house clothes, a pair of jogging pants and a T-shirt labeled "Eat Succotash." Bop puzzled over the message every time he saw her with the T-shirt on.

She had another favorite that he felt he understood—"It must be jam 'cause jelly don't shake like this."

She headed from the bedroom to the kitchen to "bang some pots together," as Uncle David passed her in the hall-way, on his way to put *his* house clothes on, a pair of flip flops, a pair of cutoff jeans, and a sweatshirt.

"We heard about that stuff on the radio, coming in. What's happening now?"

Aunt Lu was in the kitchen bangin' pots together, which meant on this particular evening steaks, baked potatoes, string beans with ham hocks, boiled corn with "plenny but-ter," huge steins of Pepsi, and apple cobbler for dessert, with or without ice cream.

Bop smiled, sipped his beer, listening to the familiar kitchen sounds.

"Well, looks like L.A. is about to get a real hotfoot."

Uncle David tripped through the kitchen for a quick ham sandwich to tide him over till dinner and slumped into his study TV chair for his nightly commentary on the news.

"Now they knew that was gon' to happen. I almost think it was planned."

Bop stared at his uncle across the room for a minute. The brother could be somewhat contradictory at times. There were times when he sounded anti-African-American (he still said "niggers" a lot), but his actions blew holes in his words. He gave money to African-American educational funds, supported a number of black-oriented charity agencies, and was generally open to any legitimate black grievance, but his fund of "niggerizations" was vast and deep.

"What makes you think it was planned, Unc?"

"Hell, just look at the pattern; them ain't no random fires being set. We're lookin' at pros at work. See how the fire is being sucked into that building?"

Bop stared at the huge department store on Vermont and Manchester burning.

"See the way that fire burning? If you just had a bunch o' silly niggers flingin' bottles fulla cleanin' fluid in there you'd have a spotty fire. Them is real fires with fire storms set off from the center."

Bop couldn't really figure out exactly what his uncle was talking about, but he could see the effect. "Yeahhh, I see what you mean."

Thirty-five minutes later…. "C'mon eat, honey. Bop, I know you don't want none of this meat food, do you?"

"I ate awready, Aunt Lu. I walked down to the Thai place and had some noodles."

Uncle David rolled his eyes to the ceiling on his way to the kitchen table. He didn't have a lot of regard for a man who would turn down a fair-sized porterhouse steak.

Aunt Lu echoed her husband's thought with her secret chuckle. "Keep on eatin' them noodles 'n your eyes gonna get slanted."

They shared the usual laugh about their nephew's eating habits. The laughter was their way of telling him, "We're for you, even if you eat noodles."

He felt half an urge to talk to them once again about the benefits of proper diet, something he had picked up from one of the hippest and wisest dudes he'd ever met. They

15

pulled up on each other in the Chino minimum security facility iron yard.

"Now just look at these idiots, Bop; they're pumping iron like it's going outta style. Look at BoBo over there, got muscles between his thumbs and forefingers, but he'll probably drop dead from a heart attack, eating all the grease he eats. I've seen the fool smear lard on white bread."

"Chester, what's this big thing you got with food, man? A hamburger is a fuckin' hamburger!"

"That's what you think, young blood. Pull some of that ghetto snot out of your ears 'n listen up. I got a little-brother-place in my heart for you 'cause I don't really think you're dumb as the rest of these funky chumps."

"What's that mean?"

"It means that I don't think you want to spend most of your life in jail."

"Like you?"

"Yeahhh, be cruel, if you want to, yeahhh, like me."

"Sorry, man, I didn't mean…."

"Aint no thang."

Daily, with practically nothing to do but talk and pump a little iron, Chester rapped and Bop began to listen.

"Most of the brothers and the Mexicans in here is half crazy from the shit they've been loading their systems up with for years. I don't feel qualified to talk too much about our Latino friends, but I *know* what we been eatin' since 1619 is fucked up."

Chester L. Simmons, ex-con man, ex-pimp, ex-ex-ex, managed to convince Clyde Johnson, aka "Bop Daddy," that there was a racist plot behind the pushing of sugar, grease, drugs, and assorted chemicals into the African-American communities across the United States.

"What's this shit with 'fast foods' in our communities?! It's like we don't have time to sit down 'n eat. Most of us ain't got nothin' but time; we ain't got no jobs to rush to.

"Isn't that interesting? The white boy is dead on the go, phone in the car, ready to go, but you don't see him grabbing those killer burgers and loading up on junk food. We spend the same money he spends, buying synthetic shit that don't do nothing but make you have a cravin'.

"Check it out, youngblood. Put enough sugar in your tank and it won't run. You'll think it's runnin' but it's just an illusion. Everything they push in our communities is sweet, I think it's a clever way to get us to swallow some bitter shit. I had a couple junkie chumps give me some sweet gin one time. You believe that?"

Bop tried to argue the point a few times but gave up; Chester's logic was tight.

"I ain't got nothing against eating meat; it's what you're eating in the meat that fucks me up. It's got to be some powerful chemicals they're using to blow a damn cow up to adult size in four months. Or is it three?

"And I'm not one of these funky chumps who believes that vegetables don't scream 'n cry when we cut and kill them too. It's just a matter of biology; I'd rather kill a tomato, which doesn't have a heart like mine or a liver, or a dick, than kill a cow."

Chester ate seafood when it was available (either legally or illegally) and vegetables (undercooked by demand) and only smoked marijuana for his holidays.

"That firewater ain't nothing but some chemicals them bastards done stirred up in a vat. Herb is from Mother Earth."

Chester L. Simmons was the man who made him understand that white bread wasn't really wonderful and that he ought to pay the Motherland a visit.

17

* * * * *

Bop sprawled in front of the television, finishing off the last Beck's and smoking a joint, marijuana sheen in his eyes, fascinated by the Watts Riot of '92. Uncle David and Aunt Lu had watched an hour of it after dinner and decided to watch the TV in their bedroom.

"Ain't no doubt in my mind how this shit is gon' come out. Niggers gon' lose again."

Bop opened the sliding glass door and stepped out into the yard. He felt the veins in his forehead throbbing. The brothers were firing it up. He could hear distant sirens and imagined that he could smell smoke.

That's for Rodney King, Benny Powell, Clarence Chance, Latasha Hawlins, the racist pre-New Year's sweeps through the project to arrest the brothers the police *thought* would fire their pistols on New Year's, for flooding South Central L.A. with crack, for making men lie on the ground, their initiation into humiliation, for no jobs, for hopelessness, for the secret promotion of gang warfare by the Los Angeles Police Department, for sheer racism.

Bop felt a level of agreement with his uncle concerning the Korean merchant burnout.

"I don't see why they burnin' up their stores."

"'Cause they're nasty, disrespectful, and rude."

"Then why shop in their stores? Shit, if you didn't shop in their damn stores for a week, they'd become very respectful and courteous. Or else they'd go somewhere else quick!"

He took a final hit on the joint and popped the roach into his mouth, gulped it down with a swallow of beer.

Bone had called back twice.

"Bop, you should be down in the 'hood now; home, these motherfuckers is loadin' up on shit!"

Skateboard tried to lure him down into it with promises…. "I promise you this, man; if you tripped through here right now, you could pick up VCRs, booze, anything you want. I promise you mo' shit than you ever had…."

He was tempted but didn't feel compelled. *This is a fucking setup. Once the fire dies down, niggers is gon' pay for this and I'm gon' be in Ghana, West Africa.*

He stutter-stepped back into the living room. The analysts were analyzing the analysts; the pundits were punditing; the sociologists were sociologizing; the urbanologists were making money; people were being interviewed.

A young black man with his Raiders cap on sideways summed it up. "If you have to ask me why this happened 'cause you really don't know, then my daddy was right, white folks is a bunch o' dumb motherfuckers!"

It came as close to being live television as it would ever be. Profane statements skipped past the censors, and the media's desperate need to be first with the latest tragedy gave a party atmosphere to the news.

"Tom, what's that burning over there?"

"Well, Jerry, that's the warehouse that we pointed out to you earlier. The fire department hasn't been able to get to it yet."

He remoted the television off, after having learned that most of the television newscasters were racist-thinking ("They're savages. Who would do this to a city?") and that the city was likely to be placed under a curfew and that the National Guard might be sent in.

Bop staggered up the hall to his bedroom, flopped across the bed for a few minutes. *Damn! I hope this don't fuck with my shit!*

He slid off the bed and fumbled through the top drawer of his bedside night table. He pulled the miniature briefcase from underneath a pile of socks and shorts, stared at

19

the briefcase for a moment, and finally opened it.

My yellow-fever card, my passport, my plane ticket, my trip to Africa, with a thousand ol' nasty drug-saved dollars to spend.

He opened the yellow-fever card and studied the entry— *this is the one that made me feel like I had the flu for a week.*

"Now, I have to explain, Mr. Johnson; about seven to ten days from now, you'll begin to experience yellow fever symptoms. Don't be alarmed. That is what this shot is all about."

He flipped the passport open and studied his picture. *What the fuck would you call a motherfucker who looked like this?*

He stumbled over to the dresser, to stare at himself. *Well, I ain't ugly. But I ain't pretty neither.* He pulled his T-shirt off and studied his top half. Pumping iron had put a physique on his five-foot-eight-inch frame. He had stopped pumping iron after his first year in Chino, upon the advice of Brother Simmons.

"Ain't no need to try to look like a gorilla, Bop, unless you intend to spend the rest of your life guarding your asshole in jail. Look around you; look at the dudes with the lats 'n pecs. Most of 'em are so musclebound they can't even turn their heads unless they turn their shoulders. If that ain't bad enough, there are two other downsides; number one, all that excess mass is gonna turn to flab unless you pump for the rest of your life. Number two, the police are gonna harass your ass all over South Central "EL-A" and beyond 'cause they can tell, just from looking at you all buffed up, that you just got outta jail."

Bop's attention was drawn to the large, neatly rounded keloid in his left side. "The bullet could've caused a lot of damage, a lot of damage. You could've suffered a spinal cord injury. You're lucky, young man, don't push it."

Twenty-one years old, been seriously shot once, been beaten and left for dead once, skull fractured, right ankle fractured by a baseball bat, in and out of some kind of penal institution for the past eleven years. Ex-drug-addict/pusher, ex-war-lord counselor of the Bricks, one of the biggest, best organized, and most brutal of the "EL-A" gangs.

Bop threw the gang sign at himself in the mirror—a Brick! *How many could say that they had "retired" from the Bricks?*

He closed the passport and flopped back on the bed to stare up at the light in the ceiling. Retired. Going to Africa. It didn't seem real.

How can I be a "retired" Brick? What the hell am I going to Africa for?

The two people closest to him, Uncle David and Aunt Lulu, couldn't really figure it out either, the part about him going to Africa. They put it in the same category as noodle-and-wheat-germ eating.

Uncle David: "Well, Bop, I tell you the way I feel about it. It's your life and you can do what you want with it. But, for my money, I wouldn't be going nowhere as fucked up as Africa is."

"Unc, Ghana is just one country in Africa, you can't condemn the whole continent."

"Tell me something, Bop...?"

"Yeah?"

"How many of those countries over there—'sides South Africa, and we know how fucked that was, and still is to a certain extent—how many of those countries are completely self supporting?"

"Unc, that ain't really the point."

"Well, what's the point?"

"Now, Dave, don't be so hard on the boy. Bop, you want

21

to go to Africa. What're you gon' do over there?

What're you gonna do over there? What're you gonna do over there? What're you gonna do over there? What...? OK, Chester, answer that one for me. You told me why I should go and what I would find but you supply the answer to that one. What're you gonna do over there?

"Bop, listen to me, I been around the world three times, done had six bitches, three wives, and half a dozen children. I've shot dope, drank all the firewater I could, over-extended my spiritual credit card, felt every emotion a funky chump could feel. I have only one regret."

"Chester, you have a regret? Hold on a minute, let me put this fuckin' barbell down. Chester Simmons regrets something?"

"That's right. I went to Ghana right after Nkrumah came to power...."

Chester was always dropping funny names on his head.... Nkrumah, Lumumba, Fanon, Mao, Che Guevara, Nasser, Jung, Hannibal, Nzingha, Langston Hughes, Chano Pozo, Duke Ellington, Nat Turner, Denmark Vesey, L'Ouverture, Jack Johnson, Miles Davis, Dizzy Gillespie, Monk, Bird, Lady Day....

"I had the money from a game that I had just run and I couldn't think of anything better to do than go check my roots. Ghana had an ancestral pull on me, you know what I mean?"

Bop nodded. *What else was there to do?*

"I don't want to take you through the political scene; that was weird. What I discovered was our people, or rather I should say, the essence of our people. It would be like going to the moon and finding out that you belonged there. I had always been led to believe that the African at home was a savage motherfucker with a bone in his nose, standing around a big pot with some missionaries in it, waiting for

22

them to boil. Lots of crazy shit like that."

"Where's the regret part? That's what I wanna hear."

"I regret that I didn't stay over there; if I had I wouldn't be doin' time right now."

They often talked about Africa after that, about the politics, about the customs, but it always came back down to the people.

"They're the best human beings, pound for pound, that I've ever known, Bop Daddy, the best. You oughta go check 'em out before you get your ass slaughtered out there in them mean streets."

Yeahh, Chester, you told me to go and how to get there, but what am I gonna do over there?

Fuck it, I'll decide that when I get there. I got eight grand to blow, I can do anything.

2

He woke up at daybreak, stared at the gleaming light bulb for a few minutes, and went back to sleep.

9.00 A.M., the phone ringing. *Awwww shit! Just when I was about to get into that third dream.* He stumbled out of bed, going to the phone, pulling the cake from his crotch.

"Yeah?"

"Bop?"

"Yeah, what's happenin'?"

"Wake up, man, this is Greg."

"Yeah yeah yeah, I know who it is; what's going on?"

"Over here, everything…. Watch that, motherfucker!"

Bop could clearly hear sirens in the distance beyond their conversation and a commotion closer up.

"Greg?"

"Yeah, what?"

"Fuck you callin' me for, man?"

"Aw, it's happening, man, it's happenin'; you can get what you want just by walkin' in and pickin' it up. It's happenin'."

Bop could tell that Greg was drugged *and* drunk. He was always drugged *and* drunk, but he'd do anything for a fellow Brick.

"So, you got all the goodies, huh?"

"Whatever you want, brother, I got it; OK, home?"

"Yeah, Greg, I hear you. Be talking to you, later."

He hung up the phone and did a stretch-yawn. Uncle and Aunt gone since 6:00 A.M.; he had the whole day to drink beer and smoke herb. *What do I want to do today?*

Maybe I'll call Justine up and have her to come over here 'n play with my jones for a couple hours. Nawww, she'll be in my face for two days if I give her a couple hours.

He strolled to the fridge for a sandwich and a glass of Pepsi. *Fuck you, Chester.... Man does not like wheat germ alone.* He made a ham sandwich and filled up one of Uncle David's Jolly Giant plastic glasses with Pepsi and ice.

He sat at the kitchen table munching on his sandwich and staring out of the window. The section of Torrance that they lived in was like a dead city. People drove up, popped out of their cars, mowed their lawns on Saturday mornings, and kept extremely low profiles. The whites in the neighborhood were showing some signs of anxiety about the recent trickle of Koreans, but there were no overt jitters.

Wonder what Ghana is gonna be like? Nothing like this, I hope.

He had two large bags fully packed and an L.A. Gear gym bag set to go. May 4th, 1992, 8:45 P.M. was git-off time.

He took a full swallow of the soda, enjoying the carbonated buzz, feeding on the residual high from last night's herb.

Got to get some more of that.

May 2nd, two more days before I leave....

Stupid assholes! Why in the fuck would they have to shoot two babies? He had lost count of the number of older children who had lost their lives in the crossfires of the war between the Bricks and the Keymen, the Bricks' major rivals for a drug turf that overlapped.

He stared at the anorexic white woman who seemed to jog around the neighborhood night and day, dumb bitch.

Yeahh, that's what did it, the babies being killed. It touched a chord in him that he hadn't know about before. He called a Brick session to get to the bottom of matters.

"Who shot the babies? If it was a Brick, he's gon' get a major-league Brick ass-kickin' and we'll take a vote to push him off a four-story buildin'. Who shot the babies?!"

All of the members denied being guilty; no one wanted to take the blame for killing a one-year-old and an eighteen-month-old, but he realized, from the odd looks that many of the Bricks gave him, that they thought he was showing a sign of weakness to be voicing concern about innocent bystanders being blown away.

Skateboard put a few words in his ear about the situation. "Uhhh lookahere, Bop, everybody feel bad about the two babies gettin' killed 'n shit, but we feel even worse about Lil Looie and Bim Bam gettin' shot up 'n shit. What we gon' do about that?"

Chester was right.... "Go on back out there and get into it if you want to, Bop. Just remember, it's an endless fuckin' cycle. They got tribes in the Amazon who've made peace after centuries of feuding to join forces against the European invasion. What you youngbloods oughta be doin' is making peace and not war, 'cause the police is *your* European invasion."

An endless fuckin' cycle. A Keyman for a Brick, a Brick for a Keyman. The prize was many city blocks of drug-addict territory.

Bop smiled, thinking about the story he had heard from an elder Brick (thirty-two years old) about how the Bricks got started. "The brother who started us up was a dude named Tojo; his father was a contractor—this was way back in the seventies—so he decided that the 'Bricks'

26

would be a good name for us. Some rogue Keymen got hold of Tojo one night and ran some cars over his head, smashed his head flat as a pancake. That was the thang that took us up against the Keymen, and then, you know, when we started building our drug scene, it got even more intense."

An endless fuckin' cycle.

The wall telephone behind him rang once, twice, five times. *Probably them fools running round down there in the 'hood actin' crazy.*

The thought of the riot forced him away from day-dreaming at the kitchen table.

"We're looking at fresh fires being set here every hour. Looting, as you can see, is taking place in the Thrifty store right behind me."

"Jerry, you think you could talk to one of the people looting that store and ask him a few questions."

"Sure; uhhh, young man! Young man! How're you going to feel tomorrow...?"

"Feel tomorrow...?

"I don't know how to say it in Spanish...."

"I speak *Ingles.*"

"Good, my question is, how're you going to feel tomorrow about what you're doing today?"

"Whot's tomorrow got to do wid eet?"

"I beg your pardon?"

"Whot's wrong, meester, you on television 'n you don't speak *Ingles*?"

"Thank you for your comments, sir. As you just saw Pam, Bob, that's the prevailing sentiment here. Loot today and devil take tomorrow. Back to you in the studio."

Bop frowned at the white people making glib racist commentary and remoted a channel change. Dirty-racist-dog-motherfuckers. *Let's see what these other assholes are talking about.*

27

Channel 7. "The mayor has declared a ten P.M. 'til six A.M. curfew for the following areas; please take note."

He was surprised to see Beverly Hills listed. *Uhh huh, I see what the game is. Just in case the brothers happen to stumble through, they can jack us up on the curfew.*

"The National Guard has been called in and they are taking up positions in key sectors of the city. The city's police chief, Daryl Gates...."

Bop flicked to another channel.

"Now let me clearly understand you on this point, Mr. Robinson; you're saying that the chief of police, Daryl Gates, deliberately allowed this situation to get out of hand in order to embarrass the mayor. Seems to me that's making political capital out of a situation that...."

Flick.

"What the power infrastructure of this city has to understand is that this situation was not triggered by the beating of Rodney King alone; that's something that's been taking place over a long time...."

"Now just a minute, Mr. X, are you saying that the Los Angeles police department has been guilty of this kind of behavior and nothing was ever done about it?"

"Not only has this sort of brutality been practiced by the L.A.P.D., it has been condoned, sometimes overtly but always covertly, since the creation of the L.A.P.D."

Flick.

"We've got a big one here, Pam. As you can see, the whole structure is burning. So far as we know, no one has been injured in any of these fires, but we can definitely say, at this point, that the Korean businessmen of South Central Los Angeles have suffered heavy losses."

Bop slumped into his uncle's favorite chair. Another sunny day in Torrance, while South Central "El-A" was burning up. *What a helluva scene. One half of the city is*

28

burning, people are raiding grocery stores, bizarre shit is happening, and they got it all on TV.

After an hour of flicking back and forth he decided to smoke a joint.

May 3rd, tomorrow, I'm outta here; may as well get high. He strolled to his room with the sound of the newscasters following him. "The National Guard has been called in, and there appears to be a downturn in the number of fires, Pam, is that what we're seeing here?"

"Yes, Tom, I think we can definitely say that there are fewer fires being set, but I don't think we've turned the bend in the road yet. President Bush, in his address to the nation, said...."

Fuck Bush.

Bop sat in front of the TV, rolling up joints from the last grams of his stash.

Flick...flick...flick...flick...smoke...smoke...smoke....

Uncle David and Aunt Lulu pulling into the driveway surprised him. *Damn! Four o'clock already.*

They lumbered in, hauling bags of groceries.

"What they doin' now?"

Aunt Lu stood next to him with her fists on her hips, a characteristic pose, ignoring the sour-sweet incense of the marijuana he had just smoked. They had a hands-off attitude towards his habits, so long as he didn't bring off-beat characters into the house.

"Same-o same-o. Looks like somebody has proven a point; they ain't happy."

Uncle David paused in front of the TV for a moment, glared at the screen, and shuffled off to change into his house clothes. Aunt Lulu placed the steaks in the freezer, stashed the ground beef, pulled out pork chops and began heating water for a spaghetti dinner. She was banging pots ahead of time.

29

Bop continued staring at the madness on television, silently arguing with the people on the talk shows, the interviews with the man in the streets ("There's no justification for burning up our fair city"), high.

"Sho' smells good, Aunt Lu."

"You oughta break down 'n come on in here 'n get yourself a plate."

Uncle David was occupying his head-of-the-table spot, wolfing down spaghetti with meat balls, ravaging the stack of pork chops on the platter in front of them, swallowing it all with huge gulps of Pepsi.

"Don't try to force him in here; that means it would be less for us."

They shared a laugh at one of Uncle David's favorite jokes.

"We're asking all of the citizens of our city to cooperate...."

Flick.

"What people have to recognize is that this pot has been simmering since 1966. The Kerner Report identified the root causes of the first Watts rebellion, that the white media insists on calling a 'riot,' even today. The Christopher Commission Report pointed the finger again at some of the same basic problems, especially concerning the police, but it seems that the Christopher Commission Report was ignored just as consciously as the Kerner Report was ignored.

"How many studies does it take to show that thousands of people are dissatisfied with the situation here? They're sick, angry, and disgusted at the lack of real economic opportunities. They're fed up with the vicious flow of drugs that's being poured into the black and brown communities."

Bop squirmed. There was a time, pre-Chester Simmons, when he had only been concerned about the profits gained from the crack trade, not the consequences.

"Bop, lawd knows I'd be the last person in the world to pull up moral on you, the way a lot of these funky chump preachers do, but I got to say this…. Any motherfucker who would peddle hard drugs in our communities is psycho-wacked and should be put *under* the jail."

"Just think about the consequences of the crack trade; you ain't talking just about some goofy fifteen-year-old suckin' on a pipe, you're talkin' about families being fucked up for generations. Think about it. In order to reduce our communities to the slave level again, every means possible have been used."

"We're talking one-on-one with John Charles Clark, noted African-American historian. We'll be back after these commercial messages."

"Boy, sounds like he knows what he's talkin' about."

"Huh?"

"I said he sounds like he knows what he's talkin' about." Uncle and Aunt had joined him in the front room, carrying bowls of ice cream with them. It was dessert time.

"Yeah, he's making sense."

"Once again, ladies and gentlemen, our distinguished guest, Dr. John Charles Clark. Dr. Clark, are we to understand that drugs have deliberately been used to create…uhh problems in the African-American and Latin communities?"

"Yes. It's one way of creating a caste system that is totally dependent on a destructive source of energy. We have to understand several things at once: the interrelation of things here, the savings-and-loan ripoff, the politicians who bounced checks, the corruption and disrespect for law and order has sent out a powerful message to the man in the streets. Them who has should get and them who has not shall not.

"The Reagan-Bush white code that has fostered the new racism, livened up the anti-Semitic climate, produced the David Dukes and others, paved the way for racial intolerance, is alive and thriving."

"Bop, turn that off for a li'l bit."

Bop turned to look at his Uncle and Aunt; they were uncharacteristically solemn, ice-cream bowls empty.

"We ain't gon' miss too much; we already know most of that shit anyway."

He remoted the television off, feeling puzzled by their expressions. *What's happening?*

"Well, tomorrow is the big day for you; you gon' be gittin' outta here to go to the real Big Foot country."

Bop smiled. Uncle David could make anything sound comical. Or super-serious, depending on his voice tone.

"Yeahhh, tomorrow evenin' at 8:45 P.M."

Aunt Lulu checked her watch, as though recording the time.

"You goin' to Africa, for whatever reason you goin', and we want you to know that we're here for you if you need us."

Uncle David looked uncomfortable. Aunt Lulu filled in the gap.

"I think it's a real good idea, Bop. I wish more of our young people would take a trip back to the motherland; it might help them to have more self-esteem and pride. What I'm concerned about is what're you going to do when you return?"

Bop stared at his Aunt's shoes for a minute. *What're you gon' to do over there? What're you goin' to do when you return? Big time questions.*

"Yeah, Bop, whatcha gon' do when you get back? I mean, after all, you just goin' over there for thirty days. Right?"

32

He knew he was dealing with a crucial moment; they were asking him, after months of being supportive, for a commitment.

"I'm coming back here to go to school. I been doin' lots of thinkin' about it and I think…. I think I want to go into journalism."

They stared at him for a few pregnant moments and then exchanged their own special code-looks. Uncle David set his empty ice-cream bowl down beside his chair and folded his hands across his belly. "Journalism, huh?"

Bop felt the pressure of the question.

"Yeah. I've been doin' a lot of thinkin' over the past few months about writin', you know, doin' news stories, reportin' 'n stuff like that."

"Well, I don't think there's a helluva lot of money in that field, unless you get to be Ed Bradley or one o' them niggers with starched drawers 'n shit. But one damn thing is certain: any of it beats gang bangin'."

"Yeah, no doubt about that."

"Journalism sounds good to me, Bop. And the school-work you'll have to do will be good discipline."

A huge, awkward gap followed Aunt Lulu's statement. Bop felt compelled to fill it in. "Yeahhh, I know it will; I'm lookin' forward to it."

It was time for them to go to bed. They were early-to-bed-early-to-rise people. Uncle David made his famous walrus yawn. "Well, looks like it's 'bout that time."

Bop felt like crying, looking from one to the other. They were such *deep* people, no shuck or jive or pretense about them; they were real. The sudden realization that he was leaving the two best people in his life made him feel sad.

They weren't huggers 'n kissers, people who peed on your leg and told you it was raining. They were f'real.

"Aunt Lu, why don't you fry some catfish tomorrow for

my goin' away dinner?"

He almost laughed at the lights that flickered in his uncle's eyes.

"You want some catfish for your memory bank, huh?"

"Much as you can fry"

"You got it."

* * * * *

He sprawled in his uncle's chair, nursing a cold Beck's, staring at the riot on TV.

Wowwww, these motherfuckers is serious.... My last night in town and they're trying to wear their shit out....

"The National Guard is patrolling the streets, we got a dusk to dawn curfew on, and the fires are still going on."

"Well, Pam, all I can say is that I'm sure a lot of people have learned a lesson from this."

Bop felt himself laughing aloud. *What bullshit these people talk. If anybody had learned any fuckin' thing they would've learned it the last time we had to shake the town up.*

The longer he watched the news shows and the talka-thons, the more aware he became of how far they were deliberately wandering away from the root causes of the '92 riot.

A few newscasters gave them the impression that it was simply an African-American rite. "Jerry, you're saying that these people have done this sort of thing before?"

"Well, not exactly the same way or for the same reasons, but it's been done before. Remember Chicago, New Orleans, New York?"

Increasingly, within a four-day span, reasonable African-American representatives were being made to sound like fiery fools.

34

"What we have to understand here, which you people seem to want to forget, is that the fuel for the fires was poured on when four white policemen were exonerated for brutally beating an African-American man named, ironically, King. The fuel for the fires was lit by fifty-some baton blows. Nobody seems to have counted the kicks and stomps.

"Many of us, African-Americans and brown-skinned South Americans, know what it feels like to be humiliated on a public street by the L.A.P.D., to be pulled out of our vehicles in front of our wives and children and forced to sprawl on the sidewalk for 'probable cause.'"

"Sir, are you saying that the police shouldn't carry out the business of preserving the law, of keeping the peace and preventing criminals from being apprehended?"

Bop remoted the TV off as the super-articulate black man began his reply. "Of course, you know that I do *not* mean that the police shouldn't protect and serve us. What I am saying is that they shouldn't oppress and degrade us. What I'm saying…."

Yeahhh, I know what you're saying, brother, and you're saying it very well, but they don't hear you.

The sudden vacuum left by the absence of the television sound was filled by the screaming of distant fire trucks. He listened to the sounds for a few minutes, suddenly remembered he had one last, fat joint in his bedroom, and made a beeline for it.

* * * * *

The side yard gleamed in the moonlight. He imagined that he could see and count the leaves on the trees and bushes. The moon shimmered silver. Bop sprawled on the concrete terrace, staring up at the moon, taking delicate hits

35

on the joint, the events concerning King, the riot, and a dozen other things flickering through his dope-filled mind.

The whole scene was like a crazy movie. A crazy video by an amateur videoman named, ironically, Holiday. Just a white guy noodlin' around with his new toy who happened to catch about three minutes of an ass-kicking that cost the city of Los Angeles about nine hundred million dollars.

Plus, a trillion dollars worth of negative publicity.

The hip people knew something gruesome was about to go down when the trial site was changed from L.A. County to Simi Valley, home of many cops, retired cops, and whites sympathetic to the most fascist tendencies within the L.A.P.D.

"Shit! They didn't even shift the Manson trial outta town, and they knew that motherfucker wasn't gon' git a fair trial. If they're really talkin' about fair trials…."

A cloud bank drifted across the moon's face…ten whites, one assimilated Asian, and one first-generation Latina.

"Hey, man, you know that bitch is scared shitless that they gonna withdraw her green card. You *know* which way she got to go."

A fair trial?

The head training officer of the L.A.P.D., somebody named Bostic, showed conclusively when and how the cops who had brutalized Rodney King could have handled it. He used an old-fashioned school pointer to stop the tape and show when King could have been subdued, handcuffed, and arrested, rather than brutalized.

Bop closed his eyes as the cloud exposed the moon's rays. He felt the sparkle of moonbeams in his shuttered eyelids.

The overwhelming evidence (to most black and brown people) clearly pointed to an abuse of power on the part of the police. But the jury, viewing the three-minute tape of the police hyena attack as a travelogue, voted "not guilty" for all defendants.

The riot started outside the Simi Valley courtroom when the verdict was announced. There is recorded evidence that even some right-wing whites were stunned by the "not guilty" verdict. Most people expected the police to be slapped on the wrist, at least, and there would be "disturbances" as a result. (Police Chief Gates—better known as the "Commandant" by some people—had put aside one mil for riot overtime, a tip-off if ever there was one.)

It started outside the courtroom and kicked into gear on Florence and Normandie, in South Central. Fifty plus lives were lost, thousands disrupted. The assault on the Korean shop owners was only surprising to the Koreans....

"They are the rudest, most insensitive assholes I have ever encountered."

And, seemingly, only misunderstood by them—"We work hard, sixteen to eighteen hours a day; they are jealous of us, of our success! They do not understand our culture."

"What is this shit about not understanding their fuckin' culture?! This ain't fuckin' Ko-rea, this is America, goddamit!"

Strangely, ninety percent of the Korean entrepreneurs interviewed by the dominant press failed to understand four basic things.

1) They were disliked because they were perceived to be rude and basically insensitive to the African-American community they had targeted for profits. Some people also resented the fact that they seemed able to get small business loans from the government easily. The non-Koreans who weren't familiar with the Korean financial self-help organizations were the most resentful.

2) They make little effort to understand the historical conditions of African Americans and South Americans. It seemed that they made little effort to relate to anyone else but Koreans.

3) They were, quite obviously, siphoning money out of the African-American community and not putting any back into the community.

4) They had largely alienated most African Americans with their siege us-them attitude.

The constant refrain that their "culture was different" rang hollow. The other Asian groups who did business in the black and brown communities didn't seem to have that problem.

(Once again, demonstrating his ability to alienate the alienated, President Bush, pressured by the corporate pipeline with the South Korean government, immediately made money available for rehabilitation of the Korean entrepreneurs. The stage was obviously being set for the years 2020.)

The verdict as to how it will finally turn out between the brothers and the Koreans is less predictable than the lottery.

The chilling air blowing patches of fog in from the west broke Bop's focus. He stood up, feeling mellow, rotated his hips a few times and went inside. *Ain't no need to get too well rested for a trip that's gonna take me damned near two days.*

* * * * *

Aunt Lulu had taken his request for a catfish dinner seriously. Twenty pounds worth seriously. Plus spaghetti and meatballs, sourdough cornbread, and a deep pot of succotash.

"Eat Succotash" suddenly had a deeper meaning.

Bop took a furtive look at his uncle's jaws working. *Goddamn, this brother can eat* up *some fish!*

Uncle David had practically reduced his catfish eating to an art. He chewed the catfish into one side of his mouth and gently extracted bones from the other side.

"Eat all you can, while you can, Bop. I know damned well them niggers over in Africa ain't got nothin' that comes close to Lu's cookin'."

Bop almost choked on a bone laughing. *Niggers in Africa? C'mon, Unc', get real.*

But the catfish *was* good, no doubt about that. Aunt Lulu could lay a batter on a piece of fish that would force you to eat a second piece, a third piece….

Bop stared at the platter piled high with catfish in the center of the table, the deep bowl of succotash, the skillet filled with cornbread, the platter of spaghetti (Uncle David called it "ghetti") and meatballs. *Yeahh, maybe this is the good life, who knows?* He pulled in the fifth catfish fillet under the approving eyes of his aunt and uncle.

The phone ringing interrupted his tastebud seduction.

"It's for me; I'll take it in the bedroom."

"Talk as long as you want to, but be careful; may not be none left when you get back."

Justine…. "So, I mean, hey, like what's happenin', mister man? I know you gettin' ready to go off to Afric-co 'n shit, but you could've call me. I mean, after all, I'm s'posed to be the woman in yo' life; ain't that what you lied 'n told me last month?"

Bop took a final swallow of his well chewed catfish. Justine was really fucked up. She had finally sucked the pipe all the way in.

"Well hey, what the fuck you gon' say to me? I'm s'posed to be the woman you looove 'n shit, huh?

39

"Justine, lissen to me, baby...."

He heard hysteria erupt. "Goddamnit, Bop, why you have to leave me, huh? I thought you told me you loved me 'n shit! And now you carryin' yo' ass off to some foreign country. Why you treatin' me like this, huh? huh?!"

Bop felt the cold rush of the crack-pipe logic echo through Justine's emotional outburst.

"Justine, I'm only gonna be gone a month, baby; I'll be back."

More hysteria.... "You lyin' to me, Bop; you tellin' me a motherfuckin' lie 'n you know it! You gonna git over there, start fuckin' them Afric-co women 'n forget all about me...."

"Justine, I love you, baby."

He gently replaced the receiver in its cradle, there was no sense trying to make sense to Justine when she was high.

Predictably, she called back ten seconds later. "Bop! Don't hang up on me!!"

"Justine, I'll write you, OK?" He put the phone down with more force, thought about it for a second, and took the phone off the hook.

Uncle David and Aunt Lulu never received more than four calls a week, and they could care less whether the phone was on or off the hook.

5:15 P.M. He took immediate note of how far the catfish pile had gone down in his absence. "Anything left for a catfish-lovin' man?"

"Shit, we thought you wanted to go in there 'n eat the phone; we didn't know you wanted catfish."

Salt-of-the-earth people. They showered love all over him, fillets full of it. He returned to the feast, determined to do justice to Aunt Lu's catfish fry.

"We got a surprise for you, Bop, soon as you finish eating."

40

How could you finish eating at Uncle David and Lulu's house?

6:15 P.M. Catfish bones everywhere. Bop waddled into the front room, remoted the TV on from sheer habit. "Well, Pam, whaddaya think, the peak of the riot seems to have withered. We appear to be back on the road to some kind of normalcy here; what do you think?"

The arrogance of these motherfuckers! Let's go back to where we were.

Chester Simmons had done a masterwork job of laying the shit out for him.

"Bop, my boy, you've gotta understand how the media works, if you want to understand how America functions. That's a bottom line here...."

Flick. Click.

"Bop?"

"Yeah?"

"How do you like it?"

She handed the watch case to him under her husband's approving eyes. The watch face carried the outlined shape of Africa in red, black, and green; black leather band, too nice.

"Wowww!"

"We thought you'd like to keep African time in Africa." Uncle David sounded almost solemn.

"Aunt Lu, Uncle David, I really want to thank you all for...."

Uncle David cut his sentimentality off. He often said, "I can't stand all that drippy shit. People should do what they wanna do for other people 'cause they wanna do it; we shouldn't expect nobody to be moanin' 'n shit to each other." "Uhh, you all set, you got all your papers 'n stuff?"

"I got all that packed in my carry-on bag."

"You got a good supply of rubbers?"

Good ol' down to earth Aunt Lu.

"Uhhh, yeah, Aunt Lu', I got enough."

"Awright then, let's break open this bottle of Co-vos-see-A and have a farewell drink. We ain't got none of that mary-jew-wanna you be sneakin' round here smokin'."

They shared a laugh. Cognac? Wowww…. Uncle David and Aunt Lulu usually reserved their drinkin' for those evenings they went for dinner on the pier. The drinkin' was usually one whisky sour each.

"Well, Bop, here's to a good trip."

"Thanks, Aunt Lu."

"You sure you got enough rubbers?"

"Bop ain't gon' be over there but a month; how much stank you think he can get into in that length of time?"

3

He felt as though he were in a drunken bubble, flying across the Atlantic. Uncle David and Aunt Lulu had poured themselves a small taste each and filled a wineglass with cognac for him.

"Catfish 'n corn-gnac, now that's what I call good livin'."

"Would you care for a cocktail, sah?"

"Uhh, yeah, how about a couple bottles of that cognac?"

The stewardesses seemed to roam the aisles with liquor. They must be trying to keep people cooled out.

He made an oblique study of the German woman in the seat next to him and of her ten-year-old son gazing out of the window at clouds, endless clouds.

There's a whole fuckin' ocean down there somewhere.

He unscrewed the cap from the cognac bottle, ignored the glass on the tray in front of him, and sipped. The German woman smiled his way.

Ain't no need to be smiling at white women in a plane going to the continent.

After the second bottle of cognac, he once again obliquely took in his fellow passengers. Lots of Indians, or Pakistingos, or whatever the fuck they call themselves. A few offball whites, like the German woman, and quite a few Africans, quite a few.

43

They were scheduled for an overnight stay in London (landing at Heathrow and departing from Gatwick) and on to a half-hour stop in Kano, Nigeria, and onward to Atoka (Kotoka airport) in Accra.

* * * * *

He nodded off like an old-fashioned heroin addict every hour or so, buzzed on cognac, bored to tears after hours of sitting in one place, recalling....

"Skateboard, Bone, Big Fool, I don't want anybody shootin' on this one. OK?"

"Can't we at least fire a few rounds in the air? I mean, c'mon now, Bop, what the fuck we got uzis for?"

"Yeahh, go 'head, if it's gonna make you happy."

Gang banging. Territorial madness compounded by drugs. Crossfires, babies getting shot up. He pulled up out of his nod at the thought. *Babies getting shot up.*

"Bone, I'm turnin' it in, man. I've had enough."

"I can't remember nobody ever leavin' the Bricks, home..., not alive anyway."

Two hundred and forty three Bricks met to determine Bop's fate. They gave him a chance to cop a plea before casting ballots, marble-sized bricks, in a box.

"I don't really care what ya'll do with me. I know what I wanna do with myself. I want out. I ain't mad at nobody; I still feel like the greatest motherfucker in the world is a Brick, but I want out."

An unruly element, loaded on Old English 800 and herb, wanted to skip the vote and just take him out on the spot. "You jive-ass punk! We thought you had some heart, nigger!"

"Yeah! I have got some heart! I got enough heart to do what I'm doing! Motherfucker!"

44

The vote was one hundred and three against, one hundred and forty for.

Big Fool put it into words: "You was a Brick, you a Brick now, and you always gon' be a Brick. If we thought otherwise we'd stomp your ass to death in the middle of Figueroa and Imperial."

He was given the status of "Original Brick" and allowed to turn it in. The unruly element didn't like the decision but was compelled to obey Brick law. "What happens if somebody else decides that they want out? What's gon' happen to the organization if motherfuckers can just come 'n go when they want to?!"

"Shut the fuck up, Kinney Mac! We the Bricks, OK? We've made a decision by vote and that's what we gonna stick by. OK? What that means is that ain't nobody gon' fuck with Bop period. OK?"

Sweet people, Uncle David and Aunt Lulu. "Well, you done been everywhere, including jail, so why not stay here?"

Work? Never had a job. Never really knew what a job was. "A job is where a dumb motherfucker gets stupid and receives an hourly wage for it," Chester Simmons.

Damn, how long is their damn thing gon' be in the air? We must be outta gas by now. He nodded off again, lulled by the drone of the plane.

"Fuck 'im up, Bop! Fuck 'im up!"

Clyde "Bop Daddy" Johnson, a heavy hitter. "I don't need nothin' in my hand but my fists. I can take a chump out!"

Gang bangin', the survivalistic fear of being killed. Of fractured skull. *Damn that hurt!* A motherfucker slinging a tire iron upside your head can hurt a whole lot. The right ankle that ached in damp weather, fractured by a baseball bat. Penal institutions ("facilities") for the past eleven years,

45

on and off. Being shot. Ex-drug-addict/pusher.

The dream-memory woke him up. Ex-War Lord Counselor of the Bricks, one of the biggest, best organized and most brutal of the "EL-A" gangs.

"We are Bricks; think about it."

A Brick. Bop took a slow pan of the people on the plane. Wonder how many of them has any idea what a Brick is? Twenty-one years old and I feel like I'm fifty-one; that's one of the things being a Brick will do for you, age you fast.

Africa. Ghana. "Bop, lemme tell you something. Most of these funky chumps in this joint might be the descendants of warriors, kings and queens, royalty. Take a look at BoBo over there. You don't get faces like that unless your genetic bag has been pretty much left undisturbed. And Wadee, check him out. Now tell me that brother ain't Masai and I'll kiss you on both cheeks.

"That's one of the things you gonna really trip on when you get over there. We got that wicked white blood runnin' through us, and oh yeahhh, you'll see it over there too. The Europeans, men and women, have been fuckin' everybody for a long time. You'll see people looking like sticks of charcoal who'll be looking at you funny.

"The thing you'll notice about us is that we got all this Indian blood up in us that nobody talks about, except for a Jewish guy named Katz. Writes books about black Indians. I can see a whole bunch o' red men in your face."

He rubbed his cheekbones absently. Funny, that was something that everybody joked about.

"Y'all better be careful now 'n don't make Marivina mad; she's apt to whip that scalpin' knife out on you!"

Yeahhh, Mom had the Indian side and Dad did too, judging from family photos.

"And who is that, daddy, with the long hair?"

"That's my father's father, your great grandfather, Wiley Johnson."

"Why is his hair long like that?"

"That's the way he wore his hair when it wasn't braided. He was a Choctaw Indian who stole your great grandmother away from a plantation and married her."

No one seemed to know or care about who the European ancestors had been. "They was just a bunch of ragdog motherfuckers; who cares who they were?"

Damn, this is a long fuck'n ride. He peeked over at the German woman slumped to his right and her son. *My ancestors?* He pulled one of the small bottles of cognac out of his jacket pocket, took a fierce nip.

The idea of being so far above the ocean made him tremble for a second. He looked around to see if anyone had noticed. What would they think, seeing a Brick shiver with fear, even an ex-Brick?

What's this crazy shit going through my head? Most of the passengers were asleep, a few were reading, some having lazy conversations. No one had taken note of his fearful moment.

Well, Chester, you ol' slick-assed motherfucker you, you've conned me into making a trip to somewhere I never would've thought about going on my own. Ain't no turnin' this baby around, that's for damned sho'.

Five minutes later he was lulled back into a fetal nod.

"Beg for your life, nigger; this is the night we gon' kill yo' ass!"

"Suck my dick!"

Bam!

He groaned from the memory of the pain of the bullet boring into his body. The heroin-cocaine-codeine-wino days.

"Damn, Bop, we thought you was a strong brother; never

47

thought we'd see you shoot yourself through that kind of grease!"

How long did it last? A year and a half, two years and a half? Am I past it? Thank God I didn't go for the pipe. That pipe is a monster and the latest shit that is supposed to be colder than "ice."

Chester has got to be right about the drug scene.

"Wake up, youngblood! Don't you know they use African-American—no, let me correct that—they use *black* neighborhoods for drug experiments. They can't get into African-American neighborhoods with that funky shit. You understand what I'm saying?"

He looked out of the porthole, surprised to see dawn coming on. *Wowww! I'm getting all turned around. That's right, sun rises in the east, sets in the west.* He felt slightly gunky in the crotch and his mouth had the sour taste of all-night sipping.

"Ahhh, I see we're coming into England," the German woman yawned and nodded at the ground below.

Bop looked out onto cold gray fields.

After the police passed off from the plane, he had to smile at the way things were done. It was a little like jail. Place your bags here, open that, show me your this, let me stamp that, etc., etc.

He was simply taking it all in, not clearly understanding a word anybody was saying to him.

"Ah sah, there seam t'bay a slought discrepancy in your i-tenerary, you shan't be able to de-plane 'til tomorrow. Next flight for Ghana."

"Uhh, what's that mean?"

"You simply take this document to the Excelsior Hotel and you will be given accommodations—next phlease?"

The fog was lifting; it was survival time. He edged away from the ticket desk, calmly searching for an intelligent face that he could trust.

A cop—what do they call them here?—a bobby was smiling at him. He threw a tentative smile back. The bobby strolled over to him without hesitation.

"Can I help you, sah? You seem to be in a bit of a snit."

A smiling English cop was trying to help him out. Wowww…. "a bit of a snit."

It took all of five minutes for the cop to unravel the mysteries, which bus to get on to get to the hotel, what time to get up to catch the morning bus to Gatwick airport, the whole nine yards.

"Thanks, uhhh officer. Appreciate it."

"Glad to be of service, sah."

The bobby flicked a polite salute off and stepped away to deal with the next wayward traveler.

* * * * *

"Everything is in proper order, sah. Bellman!"

England. He was beginning to like the way they said, "sah."

"Yes, sah."

"No, sah."

"Not quite, sah."

"Sahh."

"Here we are, sah, room 315. Hope you have a comfortable stay hare, sah."

"Look, I'm hungry and I'd like to have a little taste. You think that could be arranged?"

"Certainly, sah, simply put in a call to room service."

"Oh, yeah, cool. Here ya go."

He gave the man a dollar bill, not knowing whether it was a big tip or not. *Fuck it, it's a dollar.*

An hour later he sprawled out on his bed, belly plumped

49

out on a medium-sized pizza and two Guinness stouts.

England. He gazed out of the window, a gray light glowing dully through the Irish lace curtains. *England. What the hell am I doing in England? Why do I have to go to England to get to Ghana?*

"What you have to keep in mind, Bop, is that a lot of colonial residue is still floating around out there; be prepared to deal with it."

"But, Chester, look, man, I thought you said the colonial powers had been kicked out?"

"Physically they've been kicked out but mentally they're still there."

The afternoon was becoming grayer. *Damn.... Here it is May 5th and it looks like it's about to snow.* He reached for the phone.

"Room service? This is room 315; send me two more stouts up here."

"Right away, sah."

Nothing to do, a whole night to trip on, in London, England. Well, just on the outskirts of London anyway. Bop furtively pulled his suitcase out of the closet, placed it flat on the bed, and lifted the false bottom under his shirts. Eight thousand in one hundred and five hundred dollar bills, and so far no one had said a mumbling word about the possibility of him hiding money. No one had told him that it was illegal to be in possession of eight thousand drug-earned dollars, he just simply felt it was the right thing to do, conceal. Knock-knock-discreet-knock.

"You ordered two Guinness stouts, sah?"

"Yeah, put 'em on the dresser. Here you go."

"Thank you, sah."

Another dollar, that same neutral expression.

"Will that be all, sah?"

"Yeah, that's all."

50

The man left with a slight smirk on his face, or so Bop imagined. *What the hell, who cares what he thinks?* He strolled around the room, sipping his Guinness, decided to take a shower.

* * * * *

Sprawled out on the bed after a hot shower, a towel saronged around his waist, the last Guinness in hand, Bop stared at the deep blue lights of a cool English May evening.

That was really dumb of me not to let Justine come on over and give me a little good-bye sugar. Justine, Frances, Annette, Margaret, Justine, Justine.... He kept coming back to Justine.

Why would she have to suck on the pipe? A little nagging voice screamed at him: *You gave her the pipe! You gave her the pipe! You! You! You...!*

He gulped a swallow of Guinness and washed it around in his mouth, trying to defend himself. Got crack everywhere; she didn't have to do it.

Frances, too fuckin' educated. All she wanted to do was talk about books. And fuck. She was a book-fuckin' freak.

Annette wanted to get married. Well, why not? After three babies....

Margaret Kuykendall, black, beautiful, ambitious. "Bop, you know what I want? I want a helicopter so I won't have to deal with this damned traffic everyday; it gets on my nerves."

Sex. He had gotten bored with it at twenty and scared. Sex....

I've watched bitches fuck pit bulls for the pipe, seen niggers suck clappy dicks for the pipe. Had the claps four times in one year. The last venereal episode had shaken him up somewhat because the lab report said herpes.

51

"Herpes? That's warts 'n shit, ain't it?

The lab report was in error. He didn't have herpes, only a relatively simple case of gonorrhoea.

"Thank you, Jesus, hallelujah!"

Sex. It had gotten to the point where he did it whenever he had to and didn't feel compelled to do it then; it was purely a matter of hormones kicking up that he couldn't control.

Morning came and looked like the English evening. *Damn, I wouldn't want to live in this motherfucker a day longer than I had to, no matter how many times they said "sah."*

* * * * *

On the plane again, to Kano, Nigeria (for a half-hour stopover). The faces were ninety percent black, no German women with children, some swarthy types, Lebanese and Syrian or something. Bop stared at the propaganda movie for Ghana, a village scene with a man whirling around on stilts, a quartet of bra-less women doing a hip-swiveling dance. He perked up.

Kano, Nigeria. He stood in the doorway of the plane, watching the darkest men he had ever seen do ground duty chores.

The heat that blasted through the open door seemed alive, leaden with moisture. Africa.

He felt the urge to race down the steep steps, to put both feet on African soil for the first time, but couldn't bring himself to do something so square. *Nawww, I'll wait till we get to Ghana.*

"Now look, Bop, what you got to understand about gettin' off into Africa is this: this is where a whole bunch of shit first happened."

"Awww c'mon, Chester, don't be so 'generic,' as you like to call it."

"That's a good point, youngblood; do let me be more specific. Let's start with the aroma of Africa; Africa is where funk came from and if you don't believe it, listen to some of the ol' Horace Silver albums, or some of that Cannonball-Yusef Lateef shit."

Horace Silver? Cannonball? Yusef Lateef? Chester was always dropping names. Who in the fuck was Horace Silver? Who was Cannonball? Yusef who?

"There's this smell you get when you get out of the airport. Nawww, it's not a smell, man, it's funk. It's a primitive odor, something that's been buildin' up for centuries and is finally let loose. It almost knocked the shit outta me when I first smelled it. Ain't no tellin' what it's gon' do to you."

"We shall be landing at Kotoka airport in approximately fifteen minutes; it will be approximately twelve P.M. local time when we land, if you care to adjust your timepieces."

The English were so fuckin' cool. "Adjust your timepieces." *Wowww....*

The dark, dark man across the aisle, who hadn't spoken to him before, leaned over and pointed out of the window.

"Down there is Accra."

Bop stared down on what seemed to be a random collection of lights.

It sho' in the fuck ain't EL-A, I can see that from here.

He pulled the last two bottles of cognac out of his jacket and gulped them as the plane descended, trying to remember every word Chester Simmons had said....

"They wash their right hands and eat only with the right hand. If you're left-handed, you got a bunch of shit to explain."

"Don't fuck without using a rubber."

"You gon' get sick every once 'n a while, but don't panic."

"Don't stare at shit you don't understand."

"Be cool, Bop; Africans is cool, that's where we got it from."

"You will not be seein' white folks from the usual perspective. Over there, they are definitely the minority, but you're going to see some shit that will turn your stomach."

"Like what?"

"Like watchin' black people in their own independent country kiss European asses like they were candy canes. Remember what I told you; there's a heap of colonial residue out there. Some of them funky chumps really loved the European beast so much that they became imitations. You'll see it, believe me."

The plane taxied in; it was time to experience Ghana, West Africa, to check out what Chester Simmons had been rapping about.

* * * * *

A dozen adjectives flashed through Bop's olfactory senses as he struggled through the humidity into the airport terminal; toe jam, ten yards to git back, unwashed pussy, shit, an alley on the near westside before Maxwell and Halsted street was re-urbanized, BoBo Colic's breath, funky.

"We never really smell ourselves the way them African cats do, Bop. Some of 'em ain't never deodorized themselves. You know how we are when we get the least bit funky; we race for the deodorant stick. A lot of them dudes over there don't even think like that."

Yeahhh, I hear you, Chester, funky. After the first few minutes in the bus-sized terminal, the stench modified into a more exotic funk.

The chaos seemed unnecessary, people calling out to each other in languages he couldn't understand. That took him out for a minute, to realize that he was looking and listening to black people and that he couldn't understand a word they were saying.

One line led to another line, a man in a kiosk asking for papers, spending valuable time scribbling on each sheet of paper. *Why in the fuck don't they get a computer?* Everything seemed to be taking forever.

This sho' in the fuck ain't LAX....

Bop began to look around for the easy way out.... Chester had given him a lowdown on the corruption quotient. "Everybody is bribable, but don't be too obvious, you dig?"

The big guy talking to three people at once seemed to be the likely choice; Bop wedged past people with his three heavy pieces of luggage, stood to the left of the man for a moment, measuring him. *Yeahhh, he's the one.*

He touched the uniformed sleeve with a twenty-dollar bill in his palm. "Uhh, 'scuse me, officer, I need some help."

The officer made a quick, shrewd study of Bop and the concealed twenty-dollar bill. This was no English bobby performing a public service. "Ye-ase?"

Their eyes locked, meeting of the minds went up.

"My name is Clyde Johnson, I's a friend of Chester Simmons, and I want you to help me through all this bull-shit."

The man took the twenty like a pickpocket and beckoned for Bop to follow him. He followed him to a money exchange station.

Uhuuuuu huh....

The man returned with six thousand cedis in hand. "This is today's exchange rate. I will have to take care of the customs inspector for you and pay the taxi driver." Bop learned two days later that the officer had actually gotten ten thousand cedis, gave him four, the porter five hundred, the taxi driver one thousand, and kept the rest. It seemed only right.

"If you have to come back to the airport, ask for Oxform Amevovo, OK?"

Bop hopped into the taxi. *I like Ghana.*

* * * * *

The taxi driver made him smile, going around in a circle that he recognized after the second time around. The ol' taxi driver scam. "I cannot seem to find the place you are looking for."

At least he didn't say "sah."

"It's 308 Troas, man, in Osu. Are we in Osu?"

"Ahhh yes, my brudda, we are in Osu, but I cannot seem to locate this place."

Bop enjoyed the taxi scam bullshit; it gave him the chance to familiarize himself with a neighborhood situation that he never had imagined. People sat around small oil lamps selling things.

"What're those people doin', man?"

"Oh, they are selling kenkey, cigarettes, different things."

Ten minutes later, complete with a map to the Vernon place, they were still blazing around in the dark. A dozen people had been consulted, a number of "avenues" driven over. Bop compared the streets that they ricocheted off of to the very worst that Mayor Daley had ever left the westside with, potholes plus.

"Uhhh, lookahere, my brotherrrr, you don't seem to be knowin' the fuck where you goin'. What's happenin'?"

"Ohhh, there is no problem; we are near, I feel that."

Bop settled back, feeling cool. It was a good introduc-

56

tion to Accra. Everything had been set up. He was going to have the use of a two-bedroom house in an area called Osu, courtesy of an African-American couple named Vernon, Fred and Helene.

"The thing you have to remember, Bop, is this: the minute you become an international African you'll find shit opening up in front of you that you've never even thought about."

"Like what, Chester?"

"Like people, youngblood, like people. When're you pullin' free?"

"I'm goin' next month."

"When're you gonna go to Africa?"

"I'm goin' in May, yeahhh, I'm goin' in May."

"OK, here is these two people I know. I'm gon' give you their address 'n shit. You can hook up. If they ain't in the groove, you can go hotel, no biggie, huh?"

"No, ain't no biggie."

Fred and Helene Vernon, African Americans, international black folks.

"OK, lemme run it down to you: Helene, 'bout fifty-five, sixty, done wrote a book about menopause. Been everywhere, including what used to be Yugoslavia, and been married to Fred since Heck was a pup."

* * * * *

"I probably would've tripped to Africa, sooner or later; Ghana was Fred's idea. In 1972 I was working for a huge corporation, I had corporation values, etc., but I wasn't blind. I could see what was happenin' way ahead of most folks. I had access to information that explained how the corporation I was working for, as well as all the rest of them, from all I know, had worked out their strategy and

57

plans up to the next century…, and so far as I could tell, Helene Martin was not going to be a part of the setup.

"My foresight suggested that I look around for more 'constructive' things to do, and then I met Fred.

"As they say, the rest is history. We had us a quickie marriage and started a trip through Central and South America in a miracle VW bus we called 'The Space Bug' and wound up in Ghana.

"Prior to that I had taken independent swings through eastern Europe, made a couple of trip to the islands, that sort of thing. Fred made the idea of living in Africa a reality for me. We're both creative people; he likes beer, and I've been known to have a taste of gin in my pineapple juice, after my morning yoga exercises. You know what I mean?

"I think we strike a nice balance, Fred and myself."

* * * * *

"I don't know why exactly, but I've always wanted to be in an environment where black people were in control. You understand what I mean? It wasn't so much a matter of leaving America to come to a 'perfect' place or anything like that. You get me? Huh?

"I just happen to feel that the African American, just from the nature of our experience in America, is a natural for being an international black man. You understand me? Being an international black man offers a lot of options; Africa was just one of 'em. We've been damned near everywhere between us, haven't we, sweetheart?

"Ghana opened up like a flower for me way back in 1957, during Nkrumah's time. It seemed like the natural place for me to be at the time.

"I left for a bit and came back with Helene, and we've

neighborhood joint—the Dew Drop Inn.

The people were just like the people in the Dew Drop Inn on the westside in Chicago, exactly the same except that they spoke Ga. And they seemed to be hip, in a 1970s kind of way. Days after the Vernons had left, he was feeling in tune with the neighborhood. Walk six blocks down that street to get to the high-school jogging track, walk a few blocks that way to the main street, a few blocks the other way to get to the ocean.

He wasn't having any problems getting from place to place, physically; it was the emotional thing that played on him. Passing through the streets made him feel alien, strange; these were people like himself (he saw a lot who were shades darker than himself), brothers and sisters. But they were different. Accra was the capital, people had money, stuff to sell, everybody was selling something to somebody else. Or buying. But they lived in shacks and had drainage ditches running alongside the sidewalks.

No, they weren't sidewalks. Streets were heavily rutted country roads in the middle of the city, and the "sidewalks" were those escape trails on either side.

One beep meant that a car was easing you behind; two beeps meant that you had been run over. He felt like someone coming from a place that would've fixed all the crumble and decay he saw.

The superior-than-thou attitudes were resolved by reflections of the pictures of the Bronx, Detroit after Halloween Night, Watts, westside Chicago. *What the fuck am I looking down my nose at this shit for? At least they got their own country.* And they were friendly.

If he relaxed his homeboy face for a split second, someone would pop in on him with a smile.

"I'll tell you the lawd's truth, Bop, I have to believe that the Ghanaian is the friendliest motherfucker on the planet.

61

You'll run into a prunehead every now 'n then, but basically they're just naturally cordial."

The people bustled but there was no sense of hurry; shit stank, fish smelled, a kind of corny barbecue was always in the air.

Fish, beans, rice, bank, fufu.

He listened in vain for the boombox, some funky chump with so many decibels behind him it wasn't even funny. No drug scene. The realization that he hadn't seen a rock-head in three days jolted him.

Wowwww! These people ain't into crack.

After four days, everybody on the street knew him and he knew everybody. On the fifth day he met Elena Boateng.

Who told him about the German films at the Goethe Institut? Maybe the Vernons had left him with the word. "They show German films on Thursday night. Some of them are pretty good. You oughta make it."

Outdoor seating, the film shown on a large screen hung between two palm trees. He took a seat. The whatever it was, was going to be shown at seven P.M.

He only had to glance around twice to see that this was a place where couples hooked up. He was surprised to see white couples. *Damn, I had forgotten about white people.* In the darkness he studied the black profiles, silhouettes, the pink faces glowing in the dark.

He smiled in the direction of the perfume three seats to his left. The perfume provoked that kind of response. The woman smiled back; he could see the white flash of her teeth in the dark. He turned slowly to face the screen, keeping a careful expression on his face.

He felt suddenly shy. African women were *so* fine. He had spent half a day staring over the wall at the women who passed the house. He had always liked dark women most, and these dark women appealed to him with every gesture. They scratched their asses, dug into their crotches whenever the necessity was felt for, walked as thought their asses felt good to them.

He didn't feel comfortable with women who acted the way loose women acted in the states, but these weren't "loose"; he could sense that.

In Osu, they sat with their legs sprawled open, nursing babies, selling stuff. They walked around with bras on, without bras. He had seen four or five sets of perfect titties already.

Tightening it up with an African woman would mean that you had to know something about Africa. He didn't feel he knew anything about Africa and the thought intimidated him.

He could see her smile at him during the course of the movie. He really couldn't figure out what she found funny. The things they were doing in the movie didn't make sense to him and the subtitles confused him.

She almost gushed when it was over and the lights came on. "Well, what do you think?"

"About what?" Bop felt dumb, his tongue thick. He was reminded of the fact that he hadn't spoken to anybody in a few days. And now he was talking to this ultra-fine African sister with her hair permed, a pair of tight jeans on, dark as a piece of coal.

"About the film."

"Ohh, the movie, it was all right."

He couldn't tell from her expression whether she believed what he was saying. He decided to expand his remarks. "Well, what I mean is, I think…. Well, actually, I think this is just about the first German flick I ever saw."

Bop suddenly felt disoriented, backed up on himself. *Wait a fuckin' minute. What the hell am I doin', standing here trying to talk about a fuckin' German movie in the middle of Africa?*

63

"You're an American, aren't you?"

He stared way past her question. That was the first time in his life anyone had ever asked him *that* question.

"Uhh, yeah, I guess you could say that."

They straggled out behind the stragglers.

"Don't you go to foreign films in America?"

"Some people do, I guess."

They wound up standing in the graveled parking lot of the Institut. Beautiful sister, hot-eyed, stacked, African. They stood in place, waiting for something else to be said.

After an awkward thirty seconds Elena Boateng put out her hand for a good-bye handshake.

"Well, it was nice talking to you."

He slipped into his homeboy slump, his hands plunged into his pockets, as he watched her walk toward a late model Volkswagen. "Uhh, hey, what's your name?"

"Elena, Elena Boateng."

"Mine is Clyde, Clyde Johnson."

"Nice to meet you, Clyde."

She was opening the door of her car, escaping.

"Hey, Elena, I wanna talk some more with you about the movie. Anyplace we could go for a cold brew?"

"A cold brew?"

"A cold beer, you know?"

"Yes, I know a place."

* * * * *

He looked around, trying to be cool. *The Golden Orchid. Wowwww.... What would the Bricks say if they could see me now? The Golden Orchid, one of the big, swank hotels in town, their table out near the swimming pool.*

Elena Boateng kicked all of his stereotyped notions about African women in the ass. She didn't have a basket on her

64

head, she didn't have a baby on her back, and she was not reluctant to express her opinions.

He had only two problems with her; her off-center Ghanaian accent threw him a bit and the fact that she was square as a brick. A real one.

A well educated sister, he could tell that from her rap, even when she pronounced words ("woids") in a way ("birds"—"boids") that he had never ("love"—"lave") heard them before.

"I'm originally from Kumasi."

"I'm originally from Chicago."

Were they fencing for the pussy? He couldn't really tell; her body language and the fact that she had spoken to someone else in a "foreign" language unsettled him a bit.

But she was a square soul, that much was obvious. Kumasi, University of Ghana, Legon, Accra, twenty-five years old, from a "good family," a something in the Ministry of Culture, a new-breed Ghanaian woman, square as a brick.

They were into their second Guinness stout before he felt comfortable enough to look—"What the fuck do y'all do around here?"

She pushed her glasses up on her nose and glared at him. "I don't understand your question?"

"I mean, you know, after the movies, what else is happenin'?"

"Oh, there are a number of things to do...." She began to tick things to do off on her fingers; plays at the University, cultural expressions at Krokobite (that's what it sounded like), excursions to different places.

Bop slumped in his seat, staring at Elena Boateng's lips as she talked, feeling more and more aroused. He thoughtlessly interrupted her monologue on places to go. "How much are the rooms at this hotel?"

She slowly pushed her glasses up on her nose and smiled at him.

What did that mean?

"Oh, the Golden Orchid is quite expensive, something in the range of seventy-five to one hundred dollars."

Bop smiled. Shit, that wasn't nothing; he could handle it out of his petty cash fund.

Fred and Helene had helped him exchange $2,500 for so many cedis he couldn't even count them. Thousands of cedis. Thousands.

"Were you thinking about staying at the Golden Orchid?"

It was his turn to turn a hard look on her. He felt tempted to say something fresh, like, yeahhh, I was thinking of how sweet it would be for us to get together up in here.

"Uhhh, not really. I was just wondering about the prices."

They chatted, misunderstanding each other; it had mainly to do with rhythms. Hers was off to him, and his was off to her, but they persisted through another Guinness stout.

Bop felt tight and had to go pee.

"Be right back; don't go nowhere."

The waiter practically led him by the hand to the "gents."

He stood at the urinal, watching a slow-motion erection happen.

How long has it been?

* * * * *

From that hour forward, she was like a sexual magnet. *I'm gon' git my first piece o' African pussy.*

He thought about Justine, listening to Elena Boateng promote the inevitable. Justine, mellow woman, why in the fuck did you have to grab that pipe?

"I don't go to the German movies because I like German

66

movies. I go for the pure pleasure of it."

They were together for the second time in two days. He felt she had put some kind of spell on him until she calmly asked him "Are you using a condom, please?"

"Huh?"

"You have condoms?"

They were sharing bottles of Guinness stout in the main room of the Vernon house, the fan in the ceiling pouring gentle breezes on them with each revolution.

He slid closer to her on the sofa.

"Yeahh, I got condoms."

Elena continued sipping her beer as though she hadn't asked the question she had asked. Bop matched her, sip for sip, puzzled by her question and her behavior. *What's goin' on here? One minute this chick is asking me if I got some rubbers and the next minute she's freezing on me.*

The radio was playing smooth jazz in the background. He had fumbled from station to station looking for rap music, couldn't find any, decided to settle for jazz from England.

She wanted to listen to some of the reggae tapes she carried with her in her car. They sipped their stouts silently.

Bop stared at her feet and allowed his eyes to drink up her form and attitude.

"How old are you, Elena?"

"I'm twenty-five; how old are you?"

"I'm twenty-five too; that's a real coincidence, huh?"

"I suppose so."

"What's your sign?"

"I beg your pardon?"

"What's your sign, you know, like what sign was you born under? I bet you a Scorpio."

"Oh, perhaps; I'm not into astrology."

"Oh."

He slipped his arm around behind her on the sofa, obliquely. She seemed to ignore his move. Close up, he got a tiny whiff of the kind of funk he had experienced at the airport.

Oh wowwww..., she's nervous.

He dropped his arm down behind her waist, settled his hand on her hip. She pretended not to notice his touch.

"Uhhh, Elena, c'mere, I wanna show you something."

She gave him a curious look when he stood and reached for her hand.

"Should I bring my beer?"

"Yeah, bring it."

He led her out of the main room into the short hallway where the bedrooms were located.

Damn..., it sho' would be nice to have some smoke right now.

They sat on the side of the bed in his bedroom silently for a few minutes, moonlight streaming in.

"Elena, put your beer down for a minute."

Obediently, she placed the beer bottle on the floor and turned toward him, pushing her glasses up on her nose.

The moment spelled *Now*, and Bop leaned over to kiss her. How long had it been? He could feel her softness on his hardness already.

"No, please...."

He leaned back slightly to take a closer look at her, to measure the emotional thing a little more seriously. *What the fuck is this, some kinda neurotic person?*

"Why not?"

"If we kiss, you will want to do more."

"Hey, that's the idea."

She laughed out loud for the first time since they had met, a real laugh. Was she laughing at what he had said? Or was she laughing with him?

He gently removed her glasses after the laughter died, placed them on his night table, and slowly unbuttoned his shirt. *Now is the time for you to run outta here, miss lady.*

Elena stared at him in the glazed light, not moving. The sound of the families in the compound next door echoed softly through the room. He flung his shirt on a nearby chair and pulled her from the bed by her armpits and kissed her.

He thought he was hearing himself when he heard her first moan. *Whooooo.... First she don't, then she do.*

They began to impatiently undress each other, creating a chaotic battle for a few wild moments. He gently placed her on the bed and stared at her. Beautiful black African sister. She reached her hand out and caressed his penis. He was surprised. She had given no indication that she was into dick until now.

Where did I put the fuckin' rubbers?

"Bop, don't get off into fuckin' in Africa; you'll never be able to stop. Remember, youngblood, African women furnished the world with its very first pussy."

"What're you sayin', Chester, they got freaks over there?"

"I'm saying more than that; you'll see...."

He pushed the latex down the length of his dick and eased onto the bed beside her.

"Foreplay, don't forget foreplay. Most of these funky chumps jump on women like love-starved Congolese gorillas 'n shit. Foreplay, youngblood, foreplay."

Bop kissed Elena's eyes, her nose, the corners of her lips, her ears, while his left hand massaged her right breast and slid down to cup her stuff.

"Wait, wait," she whispered and hopped out of bed.

What the...?! She tripped out of the bedroom, leaving his hands with a bare feeling. *Now what?*

He sprawled on the bed, took a swig from the beer bottle on the floor, listened to her bare feet padding from the main room to the bathroom. *What a helluva time to have to take a shit, sister....*

He leaned up on his elbow when he heard the sound of the slowly drizzling shower.

"Clyde, may I use any towel here?" She called above the drizzle.

He loved the way she said his name, it came out sounding like "Cle-day" to his ears.

"Yeahhh, baby, you can use any towel in there." *A shower, right now. Why?* He could feel his erection sink, the elastic of the condom slacken. Bop smiled in the moonlit night. *You better come on 'n git it while it's still here, sweet thang.*

Ten minutes later she tiptoed back into the room with a bath towel saronged on her body, smelling like a tropical plant.

"I needed a shower," she explained and sprawled on top of him, her body moist and fragrant from the shower and her perfume.

The condom rose between her thighs like a magnet to steel. He felt slightly confused about the way she handled him. She didn't seem to like kissing very much but she knew where to touch him, how much pressure to apply; where did she learn all this stuff?

He leaned over her body, carefully positioning himself between her legs. Looking into her face to watch the effect his penis would have when he entered her.

She reached down and peeled the condom off as she whispered, "We don't need this; I'm taking birth control pills."

* * * * *

70

A soft, rainy season sun opened his eyes. Elena was gone. The note read: "Good morning, sweetheart, I had to leave, I'm a working girl. I will see you tomorrow evening. Thank you, Elena."

Thank you? Thank you? Thank you?! He sprawled on the bed, indulgently scratching his nuts. *Thanks?*

"Ooooooh, my Gawd! Oooohhh my Gawd! Oh my Gawd! You are killing me! You are killing me! You are kiiilling meeee! Oh my Gawd!"

Thanks?

The lovemaking flickered through his mind like a video. "You are killing me!"

When had any woman ever screamed, "You are killing me?" He scratched from his balls to fondle his engorged dick, passionate memory plus a pee hard. And slowly sat up on the side of the bed, horror stricken. *Oh my God. I got AIDS.*

The feeling of the moment had robbed him of any concerns beyond getting his first African nut. And now it was daytime, the lady was gone, and he was permanently diseased; he knew it beyond the shadow of a doubt.

He slumped back on the bed, pee hard gone, mentally booting himself in the ass. *What kinda crazy shit is this? First, she wants to know if I got condoms, then she strips the motherfucker off 'cause she's on the pill. Now I got AIDS. I know I got it.*

He jumped out of bed to go take a close look at his dick in the bathroom. The condom was beside the bed.

He showered, washed his dick several times, and sprawled back into bed. *This broad has got to have something. I know she got something. She couldn't fuck that good unless she had something. Damn! I done come all the way to Africa to get AIDS.*

He wasn't allowed to wallow in his imagined misery long; people were constantly dropping by to see the Vernons.

* * * * *

The fine English chick with the green eyes, "And d'you know when they'll return?"

"Next week, late next week."

"Please, be shore to tell them that Lucretia called."

"OK."

* * * * *

"My name is Phil Mensah, I'm a friend of the Vernons; they wanted to take a look at my painting 'Black Jesus.'"

"They'll be back next week."

* * * * *

The Japanese woman came. And a French couple from Cannes and a host of Ghanaians.

And he took a walk down the rutted street and became acquainted with Patience Hlovor, while trying to bargain with the woman selling sweet potatoes on the corner.

"You shouldn't pay that much for that," the woman whispered out of the side of her mouth.

Bop turned to stare at the woman who had spoken to him. What the hell was two hundred cedis. Shit! That wasn't even a half a dollar. Cedis were like play money.

"How much should I pay for it?"

The woman edged him aside and began to talk to the vendor in Ga. It was too cold.

He took a few steps back to frame the scene in his head.

Two African women on the side of the road, arguing fierce-ly in this musical language that sounded mostly like uhh huhhh in his ears for the sake of a quarter. It took him back home inside himself.

He suddenly felt like he wanted to cry; the women, these women could be his mother or sister. He was touched that they would argue over him.

"There, I only paid a hundred fifty."

"Thank you, madam."

He bowed and she hid her face behind her hands. *How could someone with balls be shy?*

She was older than he was, he could see that, maybe forty, but she was chocolate and muscular. She made him feel that he was looking at a peasant, like a Haitian refugee type.

They walked down the street together and wound up in her room. She was the maid of this big man named Papa. She had status in the neighborhood.

She sat and talked to him with so much wisdom and love that he felt ashamed of the way he was. He couldn't for-give himself for contracting AIDS.

I didn't have to do it, I could've waited for a good clean ho.

Did Elena say she was coming by tonight?

* * * * *

She didn't show up that night or the next morning. He sprawled in bed, watching the sun come up. *I ain't sick, I don't feel tired, I like the food, but I got AIDS; everybody in Africa has AIDS, they say this is where it comes from.*

He started praying: "Dear God Almighty, Jesus Christ in Heaven, Our Lord, don't let me have AIDS, please."

Elena came in the afternoon and destroyed all his resolutions. This time she left the condom in place. Strange shit. After she left he sprawled out once again. It felt nice to lay on your ass all day; *I could do this indefinitely*.

"We won't be able to get in next week, but the week after. Stay cool."

The Vernons were giving him another week of being by himself, to think. The messenger smiled at the thousand cedis note.

I'm in a black country, run by black people; everything is black but they have potholes up 'n down the street.

He couldn't figure out a lot of things, why people were so poor and lived in shacks. He thought about the streets that he walked. They didn't have sidewalks; they walked on the side of the road. The English never felt the African needed to be on equal footing, so he made him walk beside the road. Bop didn't know that. He was ignorant of the history of the country.

He freaked out on the women; they walked in front of him like mobile shelves, their hips were as well balanced as the things they carried on their heads.

He got up to get himself a cold, neat gin from the bottle in the fridge.

"Helene likes a little gin in her tea in the evenings."

He propped his head up on the brick-hard pillow and sipped his gin.

Yeahhh, Chester was right, there's a lot of pussy to be had in Ghana. But I got AIDS. What does it matter?

By the time he had sipped through his third neat, cold gin, he had convinced himself that he *didn't* have AIDS.

Elena is too fine to have AIDS. She ain't been fuckin' no dope fiends, that's for sure…, 'cause they ain't got none. She's real clean; that's why she went to take that shower. Midway into the fourth gin, he felt elated by his logic.

But I better be more careful in the future.

* * * * *

The future was the next day and he was no more careful than the first time. She insisted on stripping the condom from his penis at the crucial moment. She forced him to come inside her as a moral commitment. Gawddd! You're killing me!

It was almost too hard on him; he walked up the rutted street to buy a couple of hot yams and was captured by the maid. A real ol' fashioned Aunt Jemima looking woman, complete with a bandanna around her head. They fell in step without realizing it; she was a safe haven.

He sat on a bench behind the main house, waiting for Patience, the maid, to finish serving Papa. It took a long time, it seemed to him. She must have a lot of shit to do in a house this big. He felt impatient but didn't know what to do about it. Or where to go.

Finally, she returned with bowls of food…. "I have some food for us."

She set it up: a low table, two low stools, bowls of fish something, and something that looked like unbaked bread. "Bank. You like banku?"

"I don't know."

He followed her lead and washed his right hand and started eating with his fingers as though he had been doing it all his life. He liked the taste of the fish but found the banku strangely unsatisfying. It was like eating something that went down before he had a chance to taste it. And it was hard to swallow.

Patience sat across from him, her legs gapped open, artfully rolling her banku into rounded pods, which she wiped through the fish and barely chewed.

Maybe you're just supposed to swallow it.

75

Patience wanted to give him some pussy, he could tell that from looking at her, but neither of them felt the compulsion to bring the subject into the open. He felt. He studied the woman across from him. She seemed younger than she looked the first time he met her. Or maybe it was just the light.

What the hell am I thinking about? Here I am, been over here a half hour and done got every known disease in the world, and I'm thinking about another woman.

"Uhhh, Patience, thanks for the food. OK?" He pulled a couple of thousand cedis notes out of his pocket and handed them to her. She had a hurt look in her eyes, but it didn't prevent her from stuffing the money into her bra.

She walked him to the gate of her master's house and whispered to him as he eased out. "Don't worry, Cly-day, everything is gonna be copacetic."

* * * * *

"Copacetic?" Where in the hell did she learn a word like that? It sounds like something Lu would say. Or Uncle David. Have to remember to write them.

Hot evening. He could hear his neighbors' sounds through the window. He sprawled on his bed wrapped in a towel, sipping a highball glass hall full of gin.

Ghana, West Africa. He played the sounds on his lips, trying to make it mean something: Ghana, West Africa, Accra. He felt he knew Accra. Go this way to the ocean, go that way to the soccer field, that way to the Dew Drop Inn.

Have to run up there tonight to see what's happening. The Vernons didn't own a television and refused to have a telephone. "People know how to reach us when they want us."

There was nothing to do when he wasn't walking the streets looking for something but to lie around thinking. *Wonder what Skateboard, Bone, Big Fool, the Bricks are doing tonight.* He suddenly sat up in bed, spilling a little gin on the shit.

Was that a drum? Was somebody drumming? He couldn't really tell if it was a drum or somebody's radio.

Been here in Africa almost two weeks and this is the first time I've heard a drum; the brothers must be slipping.

He swaggered into the kitchen to pour himself another shot of cold gin. He felt lonely for a few moments, shrugged the feeling off, and sipped his gin on the way back to his bedroom. *Africa. Can't find a decent chili dog nowhere. People carry houses around on their heads. No really hip places to go. And I got AIDS.*

No, I don't have AIDS. White people. I saw a couple yesterday, struggling past a collection of African faces. Damn..., I'd hate like-a-hell (is that the way Patience says it?) to be a white man in Africa. I think it would be like looking at the Holocaust you caused every day.

He played his head back to see if he could find a white man that he could relate to.

Five minutes later he was forced to come to the conclusion that he had never had any dealings with any white person that left him feeling good toward him. He was "Bop" to them, and they were a wall of white faces staring in on him.

"White folks, on a whole, is a bunch o' dirty dogs, Bop. That's something you got to understand, if you're going to survive in this world. Now, hey, don't get me wrong. There are some good white individuals out there, but like I said, on the whole side, they are a bunch of dirty dogs.

"Don't just take my word; study the history of the world."

I'm in Ghana, Chester, I'm really in Africa, where we come from. It's the rainy season and right now it's hot and humid.

The drumming was interrupted by the caramel tones of an announcer. *Wowww, he sounds like a fuckin' Englishman.*

The radio was tuned down a few minutes later, leaving a relative quiet. He sipped his gin meditatively. Africa was quiet. During the first nights after his arrival he had listened for the roar of lions and the whooping screams of hyenas. He had checked *Wild Wild Africa* out a few times and that's what he had seen. The Vernons laughed till tears came to their eyes when he informed them that some animals must've made a kill the night before.

"Mummm, you must be dreaming about Tarzan 'n stuff. The only wild animals you gon' see in Accra is us. Here, drink some of this akpeteshie, it'll clear up your mind."

"But I heard animals growling 'n stuff."

"Bop, it must've been stray dogs. Trust me, I killed the last lion on the block the week before you came…. Hah hah hah hah…."

Fred and Helene Vernon were super people, like Uncle David and Aunt Lulu. *Damn…, got to drop them a card or something.*

Justine. He clenched his eyes shut, trying to remember what she looked like before she hit the pipe. Fine coffee-and-cream-colored sister. She would fit right in over here, except for the pipe. The pipe dulled her eyes, shoved inches off her hip line, made her pert breasts sag.

I'm sorry, Justine, I really am. If I had known you were gonna get caught, I never would've let you have any. The guilt nagged him. *Who you tryin' to fool? Ain't never been a sucker who could smoke crack and not get hooked.*

And I gave it to her.

78

He started dressing without giving it much thought. Justine was enough to drive him out of the house.

The Dew Drop Inn seemed to be the likely place to go.

* * * * *

The Dew Drop was alive! Ghanaian style. The bald-headed dude singing into the poorly milked mike was impersonating Ray Charles in Ga; the little rubber looking Indian guy who owned the place was going around counting noses and laughing at everybody; gorgeous African batiks were parading around; people were behaving like folks from the near westside of Chicago.

He took a seat in the darkest corner and checked out the action. *I wonder if Elena comes to the Dew Drop?*

The thought of her caused his spirit to droop. The woman who had given him AIDS.

He signaled for a beer.

It was hard to pin the set down. The music was from the 50s, 60s, 70s; the people were mostly upper-crusted. He could tell from the way they talked. People in the streets seemed to have softer voices. *I wonder if Patience the maid ever comes here.*

He settled back in his seat trying to figure out what made those Africans different from the black people at home.

They're gentler, less rowdy. He smiled at the young brother sitting at the bar, trying to pretend he was in a dope-fiend nod while the band played something by Charley Parker, "Night In Tunisia," like a piece of country and western music.

"We're hipper." Probably crazier too. People wandered through the group as they played, following the original trail that was there before the group came to occupy the space. The musicians took themselves seriously and the

79

audience was equally serious. There were times when it seemed that the audience and/or the musicians had spaced out on each other.

Bop enjoyed the interplay of the people at the bar and at the tables around him. The women all looked like *Ebony* magazine models, uniformly dark, except for the yellow colored woman with the big ass who kept going back across the dance-band space.

The Bricks would really dig this. He could see Skateboard, Bone, Fool, and the rest right next to him, loaded on good weed (no crack for them) and Old English 800, rappin'.

No rap. Wowww! I ain't heard no rap in two weeks. All the music he heard sounded like some kind of reggae. He hadn't really decided whether he liked it or not. *Yeahhh, they would dig this scene.* The rubber looking Indian guy was approaching him, laughing.

"Ahh hah hah, you caun't hide away frrrom us over herrree in the corner; we're goink to have the dancing contest, you must join."

A dance contest? I thought this was some kind of jazz joint.

Bop nodded politely and stood up to leave. It wouldn't be cool to win a dance contest in a jazz joint. Something was off about that.

Darkness filled with black silhouettes stepping confidently past craters in the road. *Damn! why don't they fix these fuckin' streets?*

"Bop, you got to remember now, we're talking about a place that was devastated by the colonialists; the English were like locusts on Ghana. When you go to these so-called 'Third World' countries, you have get into the history of their previous status in the world. It's hard to go from slavery to freedom, economically.

80

"We know something about that because of being in here, in the joint. And in America."

"Take me to the Golden Orchid."

It was so easy to live when you had enough money. He felt the roll of thousand cedis notes in his front pocket.

The Golden Orchid, to be on the scene. "How do you do? I'm Marvin Shadpole from San Francisco. My wife and those other people over there, those characters, would like to have you join our party."

White people in Africa, asking Clyde "Bop" Johnson, to join their party. He edged forward on his seat for a moment before resisting the temptation to fuck their party up.

He could see the whole thing from across the pool; a rowdy bunch of white folks, some of the women with braided shit in their hair and outlandish colored clothes on.

"Sorry, pal, I was just leaving."

I wasn't fuckin' white girls in the states, I sho' in hell ain't gon' come over here and start doin' it.

Where else do they go for something to do around here?

Another taxi to—"Where do you go to have fun around here?

"I beg your pardon?"

"That's OK, take me to Osu."

* * * * *

The sun was taking the tightness out of his curl, and it had discovered a deeper fire in his skin. He sprawled on the sand in front of the Riviera Hotel, a warm Guinness stout by his side. It was easy to drink a lot in Ghana; all you had to do was signal somebody to bring you a drink.

He studied the people laughing around near him; most of them wore street clothes of some sort—pants, a dress. And they only went into the water a little ways. A couple of swarthy looking Europeans were a mile out at sea, swimming to the horizon.

"Africans everywhere are respectful of the ocean, not afraid, just respectful of Yemoya."

"Awww c'mon, Chester, gimme a break, man. Who is this Yemooya? Is he any kin to this Obatala you were tellin' me about?"

"In a way, they're all related, but we won't get into that now. The thing to remember is that the collective racial psyche of the African, at home and abroad, is not into defying the ocean. Check it out when you get to Ghana."

Ghana: this is one of the places that our ancestors were taken from. He finished off his third stout and felt very sober. *This is one of the places our people were taken from, sold.* He sat up and crossed his legs in front of him. *This is one of the places our people were taken from, sold.*

He looked to his right at the murky outlines of a slave trading post. He looked to his left at a slave trading post. The wind whipping the waves made a low, moaning sound. He could hear people screaming and moaning and groaning....

"Some of our people over there sold some of us, Bop, just the way people been doin' it since time started. It ain't no black thang, 'specially. They had white folks selling each other too, right around this time. Some people say the actual name for an enslaved person came from the Europeans who enslaved some of their own people and called them 'Slavs.'

"Philosophically speaking, I guess it might be considered a human thang. Whenever, whoever finds himself holdin' the upper end of the stick is goin' to try to take advantage of the funky chump holdin' the lower end. That's the way it's been done down through history."

Bop felt like crying. He hadn't given himself over to the

idea of crying in a long time. He sat there, feeling sad, not knowing how to relieve it, a Brick. He wanted to run up the beach and shout. He slumped back on his elbows. *Shit! They wouldn't understand what I was talking about anyway! Or would they?*

He looked at the women with their manicured hairdos and artificially bleached faces and felt depressed.

"Why not? People do it in America. Amazonian Indians watch old Elvis Presley movies. Come on, Bop, this is a new age. People shouldn't be required to behave the way their ancestors behaved; that's old and dead. People are new all the time; we're born every day. We have to begin to live our lives this way. A lot depends on it. Do you have condoms."

It was time to leave the beach; he didn't want to be seen in swimming trunks with a hard on.

5

The invitation was addressed to Fred and Helene Vernon, an invitation to attend a reception for the new ambassador at the American Embassy. "And please bring your guest; we'd love to have him."

Woww, I got an invite to go to the American Embassy, Woww....

He stared at himself in the three-piece African outfit he had bought for the ambassador's thang. It was so easy to get what you wanted if you had money. A trip downtown to feel out of place with the swarms of Ghanaian shoppers and peddlers. Brothers and sisters here will sell anything.

A three-piece outfit, the kind he had seen African diplomats on TV wear. Eggshell blue with silver pin-stripes, sixteen thousand. He sipped a cold gin and wandered about the house, slipping glances at himself as he passed the mirrors in the front room and in the hallway.

The people on Troas Street smiled and waved at him as he strolled up the street, looking for a taxi. He felt warm inside, a nice buzz warming his belly, filled with three straight neat gins and an ice-cold Guinness stout.

Mrs. Stella, his next-door neighbor had gushed all over him. "Ahhhh, you must have a photo taken of yourself. Please, wait a moment. I'll take one of you."

Twenty minutes later he had been photographed with

Mrs. Stella's son and daughter, two people that he knew casually from strolling the street, Mrs. Stella herself, and the lady across the street who had been attracted by the excitement.

"The American Embassy."

"The American Embassy?"

"Right, the American Embassy."

Damn, wonder where Elena is, with her crazy sexy ass? Haven't seen her in what, a day and a half? He stared out at the Osu evening scene—women carrying everything possible on their heads, men walking hand in hand as they discussed the latest soccer matches, small children doing the same things their parents were doing.

The American Embassy. Big Time Bullshit happening. Bop felt a bit awkward trying to pull four hundred cedis out of the pocket beneath the robe covering his pants.

He felt high enough and outrageous enough to want to get into the reception line.

If we got this many white people in line, there must be something good at the end. He shook the tall, pale, fuzzy-eyed guy's hand and kept on moving into the interior of the American Embassy before he realized that he had shaken hands with the new American ambassador.

Ten yards beyond the receiving line, he found himself on a huge terrace, mingling with hundreds of people. Despite the fact that they were multi-culture, there seemed to be a common bond uniting them. *A fuckin' bunch o' phonies....*

He wandered from group to group, monitoring conversations....

"Yes, of course, but cawn't you see that the problem of our situation rests in the under-development of our resources...?"

"Hah hah hah.... One of the things you must understand

is this: the Ghanaian masses are a patient, long-suffering bunch, but once they decide to move as a collective unit, things happen."

"I could appreciate that capability if they made a greater effort to be on time."

Bop made his way through the conversations to one of the six bar tables fringing the terrace. He was momentarily dazzled by the selections offered. Scotch, gin, rum, bourbon, vermouth, wine, beers (he didn't recognize the brands they had icing in a number 10 tub)....

"What is your pleasure, sah?" The sound of the "sah" threw him back into his night in England for a moment.

"Uhhh, let me have a gin."

"Gin 'n tonic, sah?"

"Nawww, just gimme a triple shot of gin."

"Yessah."

Wish y'all had some Beck's. Or some herb. He took his triple shot of gin and strolled away from the table. *Wonder who's holding the bag here?*

The sound of music on the outer fringe of the bullshit drew him, tipsy from three earlier gins and a Guinness, reinforced by a late triple shot. *Wonder if they got some Old English up in here?* The thought made him smile as he slowly edged himself toward the sound of the music. *Nawww, they wouldn't have none of that shit here.*

Saxophone up front, a drummer with six drums, a bass player, a man playing double gang, and another one working a chekere to the bone. The group was cookin' but no one seemed to be paying attention.

Bop was transfixed by the intricacy of the music. The drummer was a whole group by himself....

Wowwww.... These motherfuckers is *bad.*

He looked around at the multi-cultured heads bobbing, at the people holding their drinks at the port arm position.

They oughta be dancin' instead of standing around talkin' big-time bullshit to each other.

"That's really a dyno-mite group, isn't it?" Bop turned to stare at the youngish, owl-faced looking man at his side. *Who is this punk?*

"The group, really dyno-mite, huh?"

The gin had created a soft haze in his head, making him feel slightly hostile. "What the fuck is dyno-mite?"

"Oh wowwww! You're an American! I never would've guessed. I thought you were a Ghanaian. My name is Russell Franklin; what's yours?"

Russell Franklin shot out a right hand that looked like a pink paw. Bop cautiously shook the man's fingers as though he were handling four-day-old fish. *The last thing I need hanging around me is a square-ass white boy.*

"Name is Clyde Johnson. 'Scuse me, I see somebody over there I have to talk to." *Weird about shit here. People I never thought about knowing want to know me over here. I wonder why?*

"Bop, take if from one who knows. The first thing you have to learn to do is stay away from white liberals in Africa. They're dangerous for us emotionally. 'Cause a lot of 'em want to be hurt, to atone for the sins of their fathers, especially in Africa. They come to serve Africa and a lot of the Africans seem to want to serve them, 'specially the women.

"Be forewarned."

Yeahhh, Chester was definitely onto this scene, he knew what he was talking about.

Basically he got in the line to get behind this fantastically pretty brown-skinned woman. "Uhhh, 'scuse me, what's this line for?"

The sister's look made him feel two feet tall. "This isn't a line, we're having a conversation with Kojo Adjei, one

87

of Ghana's best known writers. Have you read his book, *A Time for Us?*"

"Uhh, no, not yet. You got a funny little accent; where you from?"

"I'm from New York. Where are you from?"

"Chicago by way of Los Angeles."

The line that wasn't really a line had slowly placed them in front of Kojo Adjei. Bop didn't like the man the moment he spoke.

"Ah hahh, a brother and sister from the U.S., I can tell. You are welcome to the land of your fathers."

It wasn't so much what he said as the way he said it. It sounded to Bop as if he thought that he owned Africa and that he was giving them his special, personal blessing.

Bop eased away from the group around brother Adjei. *I don't need no snub-nosed pumpkin-faced asshole to welcome me back nowhere, I paid my way over here.*

"What's wrong? You act as though you've been insulted or something."

The pretty brown woman stood at his side. He couldn't really figure out how to explain what he was feeling. "Nawww, it ain't about being insulted. I just don't like phonies."

Ten minutes later she suddenly deserted him for more articulate prey. "Nice talking to you, Mr. Bop; I must run."

He watched her swivel away, an alcoholic haze squeezing his eyes half shut. *Wowww! Wonder what her problem is?*

A return to the bar table for a fresh triple gin sweetened his mood. He stood in different areas, pretending that he was looking for someone or waiting for someone. Occasionally he glanced at his red-black-and-green watch, the outline of Africa holding the time.

Aunt Lu, Uncle David, wonder what y'all had for dinner tonight?

It felt weird to be in the company of so many different types of people and not know any of them. For long moments he stared at small groups of bobbing heads and tilting glasses, trying to decide if he wanted to join them.

Bunch o' phonies..., punk-ass phonies....

He wandered back out onto the fringes of the crowd. The musical group was bringing everything to an unappreciated ending. He carefully placed his drink on the lawn near his feet and applauded too loudly and too long. The group leader looked at him with a startled smile.

Five minutes later Bop was standing in a grove of trees behind the bandstand, smoking high-grade Ghanaian marijuana with two members of the group. These were the first hip brothers he'd run into. They clicked.

"Glad you liked the music, man."

"It was copacetic."

"Right on."

Copacetic? Where is my mind?

He was standing because they didn't have lots of stuff to sit on and no one wanted to dirty themselves sitting on the grass. The Ghanaians, he noticed, sit anywhere. And sleep anywhere—on the edge of walls, on narrow benches, standing up. They have perfected the art of sleeping. And staying awake.

"Think about the accomplishments of people like Du Bois, Nkrumah, Padmore, guys like that, way back then. They were intellectual giants to have figured out the philosophical currents to come, in a manner of speaking." It was the pretty brown-skinned woman. He stared in her mouth as she talked.

What the fuck is she talking about?

"Africanists, Bop, people who are into 'their' Africa, can wear your ass out because there's a lot to know about Africa. She's an old continent, gave birth to the world.

People will drop names on you you've never heard 'cause you haven't read shit but fuck books and your interest in the Pan-African world is almost zero."

"Awwww c'mon, Chester, git off my back, man; I read."

"You read what?"

"Books."

"What kind of books?"

"Like you say, fuck books mostly."

They shared a laugh and Chester Simmons gave Bop a list of books to read. He read a couple of them but they didn't seem to have anything to do with his world or his life.

"Malcolm X was cool. But he couldn't dance worth shit. That's one of the things I got."

Chester would hold his sides laughing at Bop's literary critiques.

"Why would anybody wanna read *Native Son*? It's boring shit to me."

Chester counseled him often. "You know something, Bop, you and your generation are a rare breed. Some of the most aware people in this world are in your age group, but they are balanced off by the most stupid—nawww, can't say stupid, let's say—most ignorant young black people I've ever known. You don't know anything about yourselves, your history, your place on the planet."

"Awwww, c'mon, Chester, gimme a break, man."

Nkrumah. Mao. Gandhi. Hitler. Mussolini. Castro. Peron. Franco. Jackson. King.

"Bop, these people changed the course of history, man. Do you understand what I'm saying?"

"Yeah, Chester, I understand; whaddayou think I am, dumb or somethin'?"

And now he was standing in front of all the things Chester had talked about and didn't know what to say.

He felt bad about his ignorance, but he was too high and too drunk to really care. He wandered away from the name-dropping with a malicious smile on his face.

No wonder she didn't want to talk with me. I don't know a lotta shit.

The lights blinked the signal to leave. He was startled. *White folks are so fuckin' orderly. Damn, we could've had some fun.* He felt bottled up by the atmosphere. They had stood around for a couple of hours and chit-chatted and drunk heavy, and now suddenly it's time to go.

He wanted to party. He was high and mellow and wanted to get loose. The party was over.

Being in Accra, Ghana, was, for Bop, something like a beautiful freak show. The colors the people wore, the colors the people were. He fit right in. Until he said anything.

"Take me to Troas Street, in Osu."

"Eight hundred."

"Awww c'mon, man, don't gimme that shit, it don't cost but four hundred. I take taxis all the time."

Bop and the driver shared a laugh. *What the hell; it's only money. Why am I bargaining with this dude over a few cedis? It wouldn't hurt me if I gave him a hundred thousand cedis.*

"No, don't go to Osu; just drive around for awhile, to different parts of town."

The driver, a small, wolfish looking man with slashes on his cheeks, grinned. "You wanna see Accra?"

"Yeahh, show me Accra."

The driver drove along the beach, turned in and out of turnabouts, like traffic circles eddying and whirling.

"What's your name, man?"

"Zeke."

"Mine is Bop. Go around the circle again."

The driver didn't question his requests; he obeyed. Bop

was fascinated. It was like having a servant. Someone who would obey you without question.

People moved like different tides on both sides of the street. There were people out for pure pleasure and people who were hard at work, huge trays of bread on their heads, fish, brass fixtures, brassieurs, iron pipes, charcoal baskets, kitchen stoves, typewriters, automobile parts, everything but human beings. They carried human beings on their backs and stuff on their heads.

Bop stared out of the taxi window at the people on the rutted paths flanking one of the main streets.

Wowww.... That's amazing to be able to carry that much shit on your head. They must walk real straight.

The driver, his eyes glowing from fatigue, watched Bop watch the people, intrigued by the young American man in African clothes. He took note of his slurred remarks and his droopy eyelids. "Home, Osu?"

"Yeahh, take me home, home."

Elena woke him up with her soft, insistent nose. She had taken time away from her job to be with him. He faced his future with resignation. *Fuck it, if she got AIDS, I got it too, by now.*

"Elena, have you been taking your birth-control pills regularly?"

"Ohh my Gawwd! I knew I had been forgetting something!"

Crazy women. Crazy like hell. And sweet as sugar cane.

"Bap?"

"Bop, Elena, not Bap."

"Bap?"

"Yes, Elena, what is it?"

Look at her—pretty clear white eyeballs, face so pretty and smooth, square as a brick.

"What do you do in America?"

It took three Guinness stouts to loosen him up enough to try to explain.

"I'm retired from what I used to do, OK? I used to be a gangbanger."

"A gongbonger, what's that?"

He didn't know whether to laugh or cry.

"I was a Brick."

"What does that mean?"

He stared at her innocent expression and reached over to pull her into his arms. "Hey, it don't mean nothing. Nothin' at all over here."

He could almost point at the moment he felt the first shivers. He was kissing Elena good-bye at the front door and feeling her ass and trying to get her to stay a few more hours with him.

"No, Bop, I must go; my boyfriend is waiting for me."

"What?! Your what?! Your boyfriend?!"

"I'm just joking with you."

"Well, don't joke with me like that."

He realized for the first time that he loved Elena and that she loved him. He could tell from the way he felt and from the way she looked at him.

"Thank you, Bop."

"Thank you, Elena."

He gave her right cheek a final squeeze and patted the other one.

"Come back tomorrow, OK?"

"Maybe."

"OK, try? OK?"

"Maybe."

Women were such a pain in the ass. He lay on the bed feeling woozy. The next day he couldn't get out of bed and didn't want to get out of bed. He felt like he had a giant case of flu.

Patience nursed him with pills, sugar cane, caring.

"How did you know I was sick?"

"Everybody in Osu knows about everybody in Osu."

"But you're the one who decided to help me?"

"Take these three together at six o'clock. And this one before you go to bed." She was such a no-nonsense type of person. And yet she wasn't a mother figure, something like an aunt. But more like a pure woman.

He flung himself out on the bed with hot-cold spells and huddled up in knots, trying to understand what was happening to his body.

Oh yeahh, this is what the yellow fever shot was like. Imagine if this shot was permanent. Two days later he was strolling slowly to Patience's job, five thousand cedis in hand, and a note.

"Oh! Bap, it's OK, it's OK, thank you, please."

"You helped me pull through, Patience; a lot of people won't do that for other people."

He hugged her and pulled back, aroused. She was such a deep sister. A maid working in the big house, required to be available to do almost anything six days a week, around the clock. This woman is a slave. He squeezed her closer and felt sad and enlightened at the same time. This is what these old people meant when they talked about slavery. The only difference here is that they pay them a few cedis to be in slavery.

They kissed but couldn't reach the right emotional pitch to do anything else. They didn't.

"Patience, I'm goin' oh, see you later, OK?"

"OK."

Ghanaian women seemed so submissive but he suspected a mad dog at the core of it. *They want what they want and will go through any lengths to get it.*

He strolled up the street wondering if the women in

Accra hadn't developed a taste for dicks because they were always seeing one stuck out somewhere.

He freaked out the first time the saw a dude pull his stuff out and start pissing, right across from the police station. Bop stood aside, waiting to see what was going to happen. He was jolted by the sight of a man pissing onto a wall behind him. *Wowww…. Everybody pisses outdoors. Little girls slide their panties over to one side and stand up over drains and do it.*

He had seen a woman with pounds of fish on a platter on her head squat over a drainage ditch, with a baby on her back.

Well, I guess you'd have to piss somewhere if you didn't have outdoor toilets. He found himself trying to remember things that Chester had told him about Ghana.

"Ghana is an old country with some super people in it, but they were subjected to an English PR historical blitz that drove a lot of them crazy. You'll find a lot of inequalities going on. Suffer with them and learn where they stem from."

People were constantly dropping by to see the Vernons. A few of them wanted to talk about the Los Angeles he had just left. The Hungarian woman with the two Ghanaian children, for example. "You are saying that there was more than one riot?"

"Oh hell yes! There was riots inside of riots. Some people, most people, were rioting because of Rodney King, some people were rioting 'cause they was just mad in general."

The Hungarian woman introduced him to well-made akpeteshie, loosening his tongue many degrees. "A lot of what was goin' on was totally fucked up. Like, hey, the police use to just mess with us 'cause they didn't have nothing else to do."

"How do you mean…mess with you?"

"Uhhh you know, like makin' you lay flat out on the ground 'n shit."

He strolled around the house naked after Magda left, mentally replaying his rap. *Yeahh, there were riots inside of riots. The anti-Korean riot was a damn good example. What made them people think we were gonna put up with their shit? That's the weird thing about America; everybody thinks that black people will put up with anything.*

"That's been one of the greatest Eurocentric flaws, Bop. They've always felt that they could dog people of color and get away with it. It just goes to show how deep-rooted racism is. The colored people of the planet have never submitted to the white man's shit and never will, but they don't seem to understand that."

Chester, I wish you were here; man, you could straighten out a lot of shit in my head right now.

He had to hurriedly pull on a pair of short pants to answer the door. Another visitor. Elena, with a large pot of something. "I brought you some omo tuo."

He let her in, feeling slightly pissed. "Where you been? I thought you were gonna come back the other day. I damned near died of the heebie jeebies since I last saw you."

"Oh!"

He had to laugh. Ghanaians could say "Oh!" in so many ways and at so many different tonal levels that "Oh" seemed to be a language by itself. He found himself saying "Oh!" when she told him she thought she was pregnant.

"Oh? You say what?"

"I think I'm pregnant, Bap."

He suddenly felt the weak feeling he had when the fever was on him. He set her down beside him on his bed.

"Run this past me again. How could you be pregnant?"

Bop started urging his elementary math skills into play.

96

"Uhhh Elena, how could you be pregnant by me, baby? We ain't known each other but three weeks."

"I'm just joking with you. Caun't you take a joke? Come, let's have some omo tuo."

Omo tuo, the soup thing with the rice balls that were pounded into snowball shapes, the blackeyed peas, the smattering of greens, the smithering of greens, the fish. The stuff you ate with your right hand. Delicious.

She had shown him how to do it on an earlier occasion, just before a monumental case of lust had enveloped them.

"Yeahh, I could dig some omo tuo."

* * * * *

Elena was gone and once again he was alone, staring out of his bedroom window at the rain washing the dirty blue sky. A lush, beautiful, soft rain. The rain made him feel like going out into the middle of it naked, throwing his head back and screaming, "Africa, goddamnit! I'm in Africa!"

Ten minutes later the soothing rain had seduced him into a heavy sleep, punctuated by warped dreams. "The police; look out, man! Here come the police!"

A wild chase and escape from the L.A.P.D. through the back alleys of South Central Los Angeles. Hundreds of hours of chases replayed themselves in his head; some of the chases were in slow motion, some went fast forward, a few were held in freeze frame.

He saw exploding bullets flying through the air, knives flashing in jagged patches of sunlight, bricks being dropped on his head.

He jerked himself away from the nightmare, grinding his teeth together and moaning from the recalled pain of being shot.

Accra was quiet; the rain had stopped and, for once, there were no roosters crowing in the rutted roads of Osu. He clicked on the bedside lamp and looked at his African continent watch (gotta write Aunt Lu and Uncle David tomorrow)—3:30 A.M.

Bop slowly sat up on the side of his bed, feeling alert but drained at the same time. He hadn't had a bad dream during the three weeks he had been in Africa, an unusual thing for him. This was the first.

He wrapped the top sheet around his body, subconsciously trying to imitate a man wearing the indigenous cloth, and shuffled into the kitchen. The mice circling the kitchen floor seemed to be dancing when the light went on. He barely glanced at their scurrying disappearance. They didn't disturb him at all. During his first week in the house he had jumped a few feet whenever he saw a lizard in the backyard. Now he took the lizards, the spiders, the mice, the odd changes of weather, the flies, mosquitoes, odd sounds of people and dogs made in the night, the sexy croaking of the frogs, the cars whizzing past his left hip on the rutted roads in stride.

He opened the refrigerator to scare up a possible snack. Pita bread, vegetables, cheeses, containers of food to be eaten. *Wish I had a Big Mac. Or a piece of fried chicken.*

"Bop, there's enough fruit, vegetables, and whatnot to last you for a month. If you feel the urge for something else, you can get it from one of these women walking up 'n down the streets."

Fruit, vegetables, whatnot. He pulled a large carrot out and munched on it. *What the hell, I ain't really hungry no way.*

He felt the sudden urge to go out in the streets but canceled the thought. *Where's there to go around here anyway?* He had made it his business to trip to all of the places that were supposed to be "in."

Elena had given him a list. "These are places that you would like to go."

"What's that mean, places that I would like to go?"

"Well, you know, they play very loud music and people do the latest American dances."

He had gone to a few of the "loud music" places and felt out of place. One of the places alternated Kool Moe Dee with Natalie Cole. Another one played rap and something that sounded like Chinese opera. He wasn't enchanted by the loud music places. *Maybe I'm getting old.*

Four A.M., Sunday morning, Kokrobite. Or Cocobitty. Or something like that.

"Bop, one Sunday, while we're gone, make it your business to get to Kokrobite. You'll dig it."

"Fred, how's he going to get there?"

"Helene, sweetheart, Bop is from L.A.; he knows how to get around."

He had gotten around. The Penta Hotel bar for gin and tonics, the Chez Mammie, the Kung Fu for Chinese food, the Bukom Night Club (in the Continental Hotel), Black Cesar's Night Club, the Kalamazoo, the Silver Cup, the Tip Toe, the Dew Drop Inn. Movies at the German place, the Labadi Beach scene, Makola market, everywhere a taxi in Accra would take him.

He finished off the carrot and shuffled back to bed, absently pulling out a large photo essay book that Fred and Helene had collaborated on.

He was wide awake as the sun mounted the horizon, slowly reading the text and staring at the pictures in the book. *The Children of Osu.*

Wowwww.... These is some bad motherfuckers here. The pictures of some of the most beautiful black children he had ever seen were easy to understand. The seven-year-old girl carrying a huge tray of fresh baked bread on her head, the two-year-old balancing a teacup and saucer on his head, the girls in school uniform playing some kind of jumping game.

He had paused to watch the game on his way from place to place but didn't pause to watch it for too long because he seemed to be the only person interested. *What if they think I'm a child molester or something?* He struggled with the socio-historical text, returned to the pictures.

Ghana is a child molester's paradise. He stared at the picture of the trio of laughing third graders with their dresses hiked up, panties pulled to one side, shooting out glistening streams of young pee.

He shook his head, thinking about the men and boys who pissed up and down the streets, exposing themselves out of necessity, the two little brothers, eight and ten, who came to his back door at least once a day to see if he needed beer or his shorts washed.

He drifted off to sleep trying to figure out the meaning of "altruistic."

Two P.M., time to see what this "Cocobite" is.

Osu was dressed in her Sunday best. The little boys and girls who wore rags and carried pounds of stuff on their heads all week were dressed in pressed pants and ruffly taffeta, their parents in shirts and silks.

Bop felt like a part of the scene with his freshly ironed khakis and white-on-white short-sleeved shirt. The only difference between me 'n them is that I got fifty thousand cedis to blow.

He stood on the corner at the Shell station, near the so-called jazz joint called Bywells, waiting for a decent looking taxi. It seemed hard to believe that some of the taxis could still be running, judging from the looks of them.

"Hey, lookahere, brother, how much you charge me to

take me to Cocobite?"

"Cocobite?"

"Yeah, you know, Cocobite Beach, like Labadi Beach."

Bop felt proud of being able to tell the man where he wanted to go even though he had never been there.

"Cocobite?"

"Yeah, you know, where they play drums 'n shit on Sunday."

"Oh! Kokrobite."

"Ko-kro-bitey? You sure?"

"Ahh yes, Mustapha plays there, Kokrobite."

It had to be the right place; the Vernons had mentioned Mustapha the drummer to him.

"He's been known to drum people right up out of their seats."

"How much you charge to go there?"

"In and out?"

"Whaddaya mean, in and out?"

"I take you, wait for you."

Bop ignored the traffic surging around his negotiation, the people gliding past with their Sunday best on. The idea of having a taxi wait on him, his own private car, appealed to him.

"OK, in and out, how much?"

He knew from the shrewd gleam in the driver's eyes that he was coming up with an outrageous price.

"Twenty thousand cedis."

"That's too much, brother; why you wanna jack me up like that?"

The driver looked puzzled for a second, but obviously understood the essence of Bop's distress. "OK, fifteen."

"How 'bout ten?"

The driver looked at a distant point for a couple seconds before beckoning for him to get in the taxi.

"OK, ten."

Bop allowed himself a victorious grin. He found out a few days later that he could've gotten his trip for five thousand.

They drove. And drove. And drove.

"You goin' the right way to Cocobitey?"

"Yes, Kokrobite this way."

They left the fringes of Accra and plunged into the countryside.

"How far is it?"

"Ohhh, maybe seventeen meters, maybe twenty meters."

Bop settled back into the passenger's seat, unable to figure out how far a meter was. Fuck it, it's a nice day. He smiled at the driver; the driver returned his smile.

Chester was right; these are the friendliest motherfuckers in the world. For the first time in his life he felt no fear of other people or the police.

The thought jolted him as he stared out at the lush, rolling green lands, dotted with huts, half-finished buildings, people walking with loads on their heads.

Always got something on their heads.

It was a strange feeling, not to fear other people. He glanced at the driver again. In the states I'd have to be on my guard with a dude taking me on a ride this far. And the police, from what he had seen of them, made him think of comic figures in old movies. They stood on crates in the middle of obscure intersections and made single cars screech to a stop. He'd seen a few "hammers" around, but no one who resembled the L.A.P.D.

It was strange to look out at people who looked like him but were doing things he'd never thought of doing. The woman carrying a tree trunk on her head, the little girl with the tray of pineapples stacked in a neat pyramid on her head.

"How far is this place?"

"Not far, not far."

A long red-colored road, people walking on the edges like shadows, turning to stare at the taxi as though they had never seen a car before. Green fields beyond. The sight of the ocean on his left surprised him, really surprised him, and delighted him.

"Kokrobite," the driver whispered to him, as he drove through an old-fashioned, hand-operated road barrier. The driver drove into a grove of trees beside four other cars, tilted his head back as though he were already asleep, and pointed a lazy finger at the gravel path.

"This Kokrobite. I will wait here."

No demand for immediate payment, no bad vibes. The man was half asleep as Bop made his first step up the path leading to the performance area. The drumming accelerated his walk. *What the hell is going on here?*

The concrete performance area and the three tiers of audience came into view. The dancers were performing, the drummers were drumming, and everyone was having a good ol' time. He didn't know what to think about all the white people in the audience. There were more whites in the Kokrobite audience than he had seen all week in Osu, Accra.

He made his way to a vacant seat on the left fringe of the audience. The waiter was waiting to serve him the moment he took his place.

"Lemme, have…uhhh…a double cone-gnack."

He did a slow peripheral pan of the audience. Mostly Europeans, he could tell from the accents, trying to clap their hands in time, silly grins on their faces, happy to be present at a "primitive" scene.

The drummers were hot and the dancers were too cold, but he felt a spark missing. They were doing a performance;

103

it wasn't real.

There was a brief lull before Mustapha and his drum ensemble made their move toward the huge drums set up on the concrete stage.

Bop tossed his double down and ordered another.

Mustapha and the ensemble shuffled toward the stage from the cover of the grove of trees that Bop had just walked through. He counted eight men and women shuffling toward the drum. The men were chanting and shaking small instruments and playing drums with strings on the sides.

They pressed the stringed drums under their arms and made rhythmic patterns with every step they took. The woman, dressed in a sky blue and forest green traditional dress, danced beside the men, a distant look on her face.

Bop settled back in his seat, enchanted by the scene. The horizon was the backdrop, the drum ensemble had shifted into another gear, and the dancer was staring directly into his eyes. He went with it, buzzed on cognac and vibes. He went with it. When the lady's eyes signaled for him to come out of the audience and dance with her, he went, followed by eight other people.

Something that seemed like it was going to have a special meaning was spoiled. He returned to his seat and sneered at the rhythmless Europeans trying to git down.

It was hard not to admire their courage. Pale, blonde, dry people were trying to do it, honestly. Some members of the audience applauded their courage when the drums released them.

The set went on, the drums reaming Bop's consciousness. *I guess this is what I came for*. At one intense point of an exchange of ideas between drums, he felt like crying. He couldn't put a label on the feeling; it was as though the drum had awakened feelings he didn't know he had.

And too suddenly, the drummers were shuffling away, chanting as they moved, the lone dancer a part of the mirage.

Damn.... That was some heavy shit they just laid on us.

He looked around for someone to share his vibes with. The Europeans were bubbling with love for African rhythm. He twisted in his seat to take in the rest of the crowd. It wasn't difficult to spot her; she was obviously the most beautiful woman in the whole place.

He stood up quickly and made a beeline to her side. It was irresistible not to talk with this sister.

She is too fine.

Small sister, 'bout five or so, built like a brick shit-house, chocolate-honey colored. He stopped next to her chair and made a French Army salute.

"Clyde Johnson at your leisure, and what might your name be, if I may be so bold as to ask?"

The beautiful chocolate-honey colored woman covered her beautiful mouth with her beautiful hands and laughed.

Bop became instantly hostile. *What's this about? Why is she laughing at me?*

"What's so funny?"

She stopped laughing to reveal a beautiful smile.

"It sounded so funny to hear someone say what you just said."

He plopped into the empty seat beside her. This was going to be fun.

"Oh yeahhh, you thought that was funny, huh? Well, what do you think of this?"

He pantomimed slugging her in the jaw with an exaggerated swing. She laughed harder. He knew he had her on his line now. She was sensitive to his Bop-don't-play-that sense of humor.

"Seriously, what's your name?"

"Seriously, my name is Nana Cecilia."

"Pleased to be of your acquaintance, I'm sure." The continent was changing Bop; he was beginning to feel he could be as suave as the rest of them.

"Pleased to meet you," she answered and dazzled him with a smile. "And this is my mommy."

Bop stared vacantly at the queen sitting on the other side of Nana Cecilia. He nodded politely, wondering how he could have missed this larger version of his dream sister.

The queen nodded back without smiling and adjusted the folds of her large batik scarf as though they were ruffled feathers.

The mother did not approve of him sitting next to her daughter, but he guessed she didn't want to be impolite. Ghanaians, he had found, were always polite. The older woman puffed her chest out, adjusted and readjusted her cloth around her body, but she didn't actually come out and say, "You can't talk to my daughter."

Bop took advantage of the cultural lull. "Uhhh, you come here a lot?"

"To Kokrobite?"

"Yeahhh, here."

He still felt ill at ease trying to pronounce African names like Kokrobite.

"Not very often. I'm too busy preparing for my exams and, of course, my responsibilities as an Ampoti-hene take up a good deal of my time."

"Am-potty-what?"

Three performance groups later, Bop felt that he knew what an Ampoti-hene was all about. "I had a position something like that when I was in the Bricks."

A war chieftainess. He couldn't really figure out what to make of it. He could definitely figure out what he wanted to do with her, but mommy was the block.

106

"Uhhh, look, 'Cilia, why don't we take a little walk?"

They were into the jugglers now, marvelous athletes who seemed to be able to twirl anything around on the end of a stick—dishpans, plates, each other.

"Take a walk with you, where?"

They were almost whispering now.

"Uhhh, right over there, towards the beach." She stared at him a few seconds.

"My mom would not give permission for me to walk anywhere with you; you are a stranger. It wouldn't be proper."

Bop was ready with the counter-punch, "Hey I may be a stranger to her but *you* know me. I'm no stranger to you." He gave her hand a furtive squeeze.

Mom took note of the action and stood up, outraged. "Come Cecilia, it's time."

He wanted to respond to her shy wave good-bye with a hug, but mom's forbidding glare held him in his seat. "See you."

He slumped in his seat and ordered another double cognac. His dream sister was gone, stolen from him by her jealous momma.

Damn.

He sat through a couple more demonstrations of Ghanaian culture, feeling depressed. There was something vaguely disturbing about watching the dancers dance for the Europeans. *Why do they have to grin at these motherfuckers so much?*

Ten minutes later he staggered to his feet and started the walk back to his waiting overpriced taxi.

* * * * *

The night air bashed against his face, leaving the odor

of roasting corn, sugar cane syrup, stray snatches of languages, raw sewage, smoke from charcoal fires, Accra. *My last week in Ghana, West Africa…. So much happened, I can't even remember half of this shit.*

"Bop, mark my words, by the time you've been in Africa a week, you'll be feeling like you've lived your whole life there."

You were right, Chester, right as rain. Did I do what I was supposed to do? I didn't make the slave castles, but that was something Chester warned me about.

"Ofainey, I beg you, don't be misled into no such shit as believing that our roots take place in a slave castle. Go deeper than that. You're young; your hormones are pumping. Fall in love with Africa, Bop; it's a beautiful place to love. In some of the village places they'll make you feel like you're in the middle of your natural habitat. The music of the languages will hypnotize you; you'll have times when you've understood exactly what someone has said, without understanding a single word. It's in the sounds. People yell 'n scream at each other just the way they do in Chicago—

"'Heyyyy maaaan, where you goin'?'

"'Ovah heah to pick up this stuff. I'll see you lataah, down at the joint.'

"You hear shit like that. It's a funky old kind of place; people honor traditions. Some of the contradictions will wear you out, but forget about that. Just go with the flow."

Wowwww…, the Vernons are home. Let me hurry up and hear what they did.

6

Fred and Helene were back from the north, full of piss, vinegar, and good vibes. "Too bad you don't have more time, Bop; you'd love the north. You know how it is when you go inland; shit is different."

Helene made one of her uniquely creative dishes, a lasagna-styled casserole with tamales and pasta. Fred set up the party atmosphere with three beers. They enjoyed each other's company. Fred exchanged winks with his wife. "What did you do while we were gone?"

Bop tried to tell them but nothing would come out. "Oooh, I hung out, you know, just sorta hung out."

Fred had drunk just enough beer to challenge his description of what he had done. "Just hung out? What the hell does that mean?"

Wowwww..., shades of Aunt Lu and Uncle David. "Uhhh, well, you know what I mean."

Later on that evening, after the mango pie, they spooled it out more carefully. "So, now, you got a woman, huh?"

Elena Boateng, my woman? Hmmmmm. "Uhhh, Fred, I wouldn't go so far as to call her that."

"What would you call her? Y'all been fuckin', right?"

Fred's words scalded him. It would've been all right to talk about the scene together, man to man, but not in front of Helene.

"Uhh, I think you could say we've become tight."

Helene Vernon saved him from further explanation with a letter. "I checked the PO box and this is for you."

Subconsciously, while waiting for the envelope to be placed in his hand, he asked the silent question: *Did they send any money?*

The letter was from Chester L. Simmons, written in a dim cell in a Romanian prison.

"It's from Chester."

"I saw the return address."

Bop stripped the brown envelope off of the three-page letter. "It's from Chester L. Simmons."

The Vernons exchanged knowing looks; it was obvious from Bop's tone of voice that he was talking about a hero. He started reading the letter aloud without thinking. "Ohhh, sorry; you guys wanna hear this?"

"Read it, Bop; let's see what ol' Chester boy is talking about."

"Bop, I hope this letter finds you at the Vernons' place and that you and they are doing as well as possible. As you can see from the info on the envelope 'n shit, I'm doing time in another kind of joint. A Romanian jail, youngblood, is not to be laughed at. But I'll deal with that in due time. What happened? Well, let me make it quick 'n dirty. After you got out I got a li'l bit antsy. You know how it is. I didn't even have anybody to rap with…. I don't have to try to begin to tell you what a conversation with the average funky chump is like in the joint. So, I decided to 'absent' myself.

"How do you 'absent' yourself from prison? Well, you just don't *be* there anymore. It ain't no real big thang. As a matter of fact, I used to 'absent' myself as often as I wanted to. I ran into the fuckin' warden one night, in a Mexican restaurant in Chino, and he asked me whether I

110

was going to be back in for the morning roll call. I told him yes, and I *was* back there..., bright 'n shinin'..., but that's neither here nor there.

"Like I said, I 'absented' myself from Chino immediately after you left. I had been looking at the aftermath of the Soviet Union break-up and the Eastern European break-up, you know? Through East German-West German consolidation and all that Euro-madness. And I got to thinking...hey, there's got to be an opening over there for a funky chump such as myself who could come up with the right scam.

"I decided to become the lost-found son of the late Emperor Haile Selassie. I knew that would grant me some entry, you dig? And that's what I did. I got my number together and swung on into it with all horns blowing.

"Bucharest

"It was pure kicks for a hot minute, the whole tamale; they gave me the keys to the palace and I tried to clean it out. Problem was, I tried to do too much too soon. I think the CIA may have been in on the bust, but be that as it may, I'm here and I'll be here for sixty-two years or something like that. I almost 'absented' myself to get down with the niece of the present ruler's daughter last week, but I decided to cool it for a few months. I'm not hurting or wanting for anything. The Romanians are like Spanish or Italians, which means that jail is not considered separate from society. My woman Iasi brings me everything I want and I find myself wanting less 'n less as I grow older.

"I hope this reaches you in Ghana and that you didn't turn 'nigger-tail' on me and went back down into the 'hood like a funky chump. I'm writing you in Ghana, care of Fred and Helene, because my base instinct tells me that's where you oughta be. I almost wrote to your uncle's pad, but I decided dabi (you should know what that means by now),

I'll write to the blood in Ghana, in the homeland.

"Yeah, I know what went down in EL-A; that was s'posed to happen. I explained to you about white folks. Remember? In any case, drop me a return kite if you do receive this. If you don't, well, here's one more bunch of words in the latter day winds—Me, Chester."

Bop didn't know whether to laugh or cry, finishing the letter. *In jail, in Row-mania?* He turned to Fred and Helene. "How well did you all know Chester?"

Helene lit her tenth forbidden cigarette of the day and blew the smoke up into the revolving fan. Fred took a hard sip on his beer and crossed his legs. "We didn't really know the brother at all, not really."

"Huh?"

"Nawww, we didn't really know the brother; you know what I mean? When he came through here, he was going a mile a minute."

"What I remember most about Chester was the lies he told."

Bop perked up. *Chester? A liar? Really?*

"Oh yes, my brother; Chester could lie his ass off."

"Oh!"

"Look, lemme run it down to you, Bop, OK? A lot of people run through here...."

"Yeahhh, I know; you must've had about a hundred people come through while I was here."

"That's the way it's been since we got here. People come 'n go, but we can never get people to do what they said they was gonna do."

"Now, Fred, there's no need to put that kind of weight on Bop's head."

"Fuck it! Why not! He's a big boy; he oughta be able to stand the truth by now."

Bop recognized from Fred's slight slur that he was semi-

112

drunk. "Go 'head on, man, put it out there; let me hear it."

"Now don't get me wrong, I'm not saying Chester is a bad dude or anything like that. I'm just saying that he reminds me of at least a couple hundred other people who've buzzed in and out of here. They promise to send film back, or underwear or shit we can't get hold of here too easily. And so far I ain't seen none of the shit they were supposed to send.

"Chester spent a week in this house and went away with a list. You hear what I'm sayin'? He left with a list and made a solemn promise that he was gonna send this shit as soon as he got back to the states. Have you seen a polar bear take a shit around here lately?"

Aside from the talk about Chester, which made him feel a little uneasy, they stimulated him with talk about life in Ghana.

Fred: "You sometimes get the feeling that Ghana is like a mystery country. I don't mean mystery in the sense of being spooky or anything like that; you understand what I mean? It has its own special kind of vibes, a feeling that you won't feel anywhere else. I can't really put a label on it because I can't think of one that would fit.

"All I can tell you is this: I been halfway around the world in both directions, and I've never felt the same feeling anywhere else that I've felt here. This is the best place in the world, in my mind, to be an international African."

Helene: "It would be easy to deal with a whole host of negatives, but who wants to do that? I'd have to agree with Fred about the vibes. It's here. I think that this is probably the one place in West Africa that African Americans could come to and really feel that they had returned home. It may have something to do with the way people act."

"Chester once told me about how people remind him of people on the westside of Chicago."

"Shit, it's true; the niggers here is just like niggers in the states."

Bop cringed at the word "niggers," 'specially in Africa, but he was mindful of the fact that he couldn't try to correct another man's language until he got his own shit squared away.

"Tell us what you feel about being in an environment where black people are in control for a change."

"Well, now just a minute, Helene; we know they ain't completely in control. We still have the usual underground bullshit happening. Sometimes I look around and it seems like the Lebanese own damned near everything."

"How do I feel...?"

"Yeah, how do you feel about being in a country where black men and women fly the airplanes and make up the budget?"

Bop settled back in his chair to think for a few moments. *How do I feel?* He thought seriously about the question. The people didn't act the way he thought people should act. There was something a little too humble about them, to his way of thinking. But there was a sweetness about the way they did their daily things that took him in. In addition to everything else, he didn't fear the streets (roads) at night, and there was no thought of beast-police on the prowl. The rutted roads and the hard work people did under the tropical sun didn't enchant him, but he loved the way the people looked and moved.

It was all about the people. *How do I feel?* "How do I feel? I'd have to say I feel pretty good about being here. That's how I feel. The problem is, I can't exactly explain what makes me feel that way."

The Vernons exchanged knowing looks and changed the subject. Fred took the lead. "Awright, fuck how you feel. Who is this woman you been fuckin'?"

* * * * *

He sprawled out on the narrow bed, listening to the dull roar of the ocean and watching Elena brush her hair in the small, dirty, cracked mirror on the opposite side of the room. *What was it that Uncle David called women's asses? Twidcutters. Yeahhh, twidcutters. Sister sho' got a helluva twidcutter on her.*

He loved the way she was built—the firm breasts, the pert nipples, the cinched waist and flanged behind.

Yeahhh, sister sho' nuff got a twidcutter on her.

They were both semi-drunk from four Guinness stouts each and a couple tots of local gin. He took an absent-minded look around the hotel room. *The Riviera Hotel, ten thousand a night and it ain't hittin' on shit. The bed is too narrow, the crappy furniture looks like it come out of a third-class thrift shop. No soap in the bathroom. A half dirty little towel. Ten thousand cedis, for what?*

Elena turned slowly in the dimly lit room, seeming to measure her movements with the swell of the ocean a hundred yards away.

Well, at least it's on the ocean.

Elena finished brushing her hair, retrieved her glasses from the nightstand beside the narrow bed, and snuggled back under the sheet with him. "So, when do you leave?"

"Friday, I be leavin' on Friday."

She snuggled up into his armpit and mumbled, "No big deal."

Bop felt instantly angry. *What the fuck is that supposed to mean?*

"Hey, what's that s'posed to mean? No big deal?" He felt that she was trying to front him off, to pretend that she wasn't going to miss him.

115

"No big deal," she repeated and began to gently fondle his dick.

Wowww…, this is a strange broad.

"Uhhh, Elena, hold on a minute, baby. You talk like you ain't gonna miss me 'n shit."

She clenched the length of his dick and applied a soft pressure as she spoke. "What difference would it make? You're leaving." The logic of her statement stunned him. What *was* there to say? He pulled her on top of him. "We got four more days before I go; let's make the most of it."

He removed her glasses and placed them on the bedside table. "Yeahhh, we got four more days and nights," he whispered in her ear as he slowly pushed himself up into her vagina.

They carefully fitted themselves to each other, artful lovers with hours of practice between them. *Oh my God! We ain't using a rubber, oh my God!* "Uhhh, Elena! Elena! hold up a sec, baby…. I got to get a rubber."

She pressed his shoulders back to the bed. "There's no need; I started my period yesterday."

He settled back to enjoy the sex act with her before, seconds later, he was overwhelmed by fear. *Blood! Oh my God! She's bleeding AIDS on me.* He wanted to push her up off of him and jump into the shower, but her movements and the strange passion she built in him with her soft moans prevented him from doing anything.

"Ooooohhh my Gawd! You are killing me! Ooooohhh my Gawd! You are killing me. You are killllliinnng me! Oh my Gawd!"

* * * * *

Patience proved harder to walk away from.

"Gbop," that's the way she spoke his name in the Ga

116

fashion with an exploding "B."

"Gbop, you must remember: many are called and few are chosen."

She was a village woman and would always be a village woman. She wallowed in her village intelligence but didn't know how to use a washer and dryer.

She made him understand the nuances of condom love.

They were deliriously happy with their discovery of each other. Life would never be the same for either of them. They had overcome barriers to be with each other. She thought the man she worked for was acceptable, and he couldn't make himself think of what being a maid meant. She was coming from so far down that even being a maid was a step up.

She quoted proverbs to him by candlelight, back in the "boys quarters." The intensity of their loving made him feel like he was in another dimension. She stared into his face as though her eyes had melted.

"Who are we, Gbop? and what made us what we are in this life?"

As the days passed each person that he had ever exchanged a glance with, smiled at, had a visual familiarity with, became family.

He walked to the post office, feeling that he was saying good-bye to his family.

He spent hours in the smaller joints; they seemed to be hippest. Women were coming out of the woodwork on him and he loved it, but he couldn't really get into it because he was positive he had AIDS. *We traded blood.* He had almost fainted when he swabbed his dick off and smeared blood onto the half dirty little towel. *Blood.*

Have to go to the clinic soon as I get home. HIV positive; I can see it right now, all the Bricks at my funeral, people cryin' 'n shit.

He was up early on Wednesday to walk to familiar places. Six blocks down that street to get to the high school jogging track, a few blocks the other way to get to the ocean. He wasn't having problems going from place to place, physically; it was the emotional thing that played on his head.

These were people like himself (he saw a lot who were shades darker than himself), brothers and sisters. But they were different. These brothers here are from different tribes 'n shit. He had managed to find out, the hard way, that the men with the slashes on their cheeks were mostly northerners. Jumping into a taxi one day he joked about the deep gashes on each of the man's cheeks.

"What happened, pal, cut yourself shaving?"

The driver thought it was an absurd joke and laughed at it, and then explained why his marks were there. "*All* of us didn't cut ourselves shaving in my village. These marks identify us as members of the same clan."

"Oh!"

He felt a weird nostalgia hugging the drainage ditches as he strolled along the rutted country roads in the heart of the city.

He tried to cultivate the Accra-Ghanaian disdain for cars and trucks that beeped-squawked once and then passed so close that he felt they were running up his leg. The Vernons seemed to be watching him from a distance. They had reached that hip place in life that allowed them the freedom to grant other people freedom.

Fred's favorite greeting—"Wha's happenin'?"—was grated out in the morning and at odd times of the day, but it wasn't a requirement that Bop had to tell him exactly what was "happenin'."

It was an option, an invitation. Sometimes he took it and spent a quick hour trying to explain what was happenin'.

There were other times when he didn't feel capable of explaining what was "happenin'."

Helene did her morning yoga, edited short stories, prepared articles, baked chocolate chip cookies, made herself available for his random, philosophical comments about Ghana. "It's like, you know, it's like everything is crumbling and funky. I'm not trying to talk down about nothin'."

"I know what you're sayin'."

"Yeahhh, old and crumblin' and funky. You know that street that runs straight to the back of the market?"

"Lokko Road."

"Yeah, that's the one. I was walkin' through there earlier today and it was crazy 'cause I had this sudden feelin' like I was walkin' through all the black neighborhoods in the world. Sound crazy, don't it?"

"Not to me."

"I mean, it was a thang like, like three or four people passed me on this real funky road in three-piece suits, carrying briefcases even, and right beside them was some other people walking in flipflops or no shoes at all. And they were moving with this kind of straight-ahead step that never seems to rush. And the colors of the people. I saw a woman who looked like her face was the color of charcoal."

"I've seen those colored people. Makes it easier to understand why the Greeks labeled Africans 'people with burned faces.'"

"Oh, I didn't know that."

"But go on; this is interesting."

"Yeahhh, it was like I was seein' all kinds of black people all at once; I saw members of my family even. That always trips me out when I see people who look like Aunt Lulu or Uncle David. Or Skateboard, Bone, and a few other Bricks that I need to kick it with. No drugs goin' around."

He felt Helene was saying something slick when she said, "Are you disappointed?"

"About not seein' any dope?"

"Yes. We know all about the crack epidemic in the states."

"Epidemic?"

"Well, you could say 'plague,' if you wanted to be completely correct."

"Uhhh, no, I'm not disappointed."

There was something about the most casual chit-chat with Helene that made him feel as though she was telling him stuff he didn't know.

He packed his bags on Wednesday afternoon and stuffed ten crisp one-hundred-dollar bills into an airmail envelope for Fred and Helene.

Beautiful people.

"Wha's happenin'?"

"Nothin' too much. Looks it's windin' down for me."

"Gettin' ready to get back down into the pit, huh?"

"Yeah, I guess you could call it that."

Wednesday night he lay in a dingy hotel room with Elena, thinking about Justine. *Beautiful sister. I'm gonna have to go back there and get her ass in gear; I can't let her go down like that.*

"So, I mean, hey, like what's happenin', mister man? I know you gettin' ready to go off to Afric-co 'n shit, but you could've called me; I mean after all I'm s'posed to be the woman in yo' life, ain't that what you lied 'n told me last month?"

"You lyin' to me, Bop, you tellin' me a motherfuckin' lie 'n you know it! You gonna git over there 'n start fuckin' them Afric-co women 'n forget all about me...."

"Bap? Bap? Bap?!"

"Huh? Oh...."

"Are you asleep?"

"Nawww, just layin' here thinkin'."

"About what?"

"Ohh, I don't know…, about life, about people, different stuff."

A rooster crowed somewhere, a double-jointed voice called out to another double-jointed voice.

"You think a lot, don't you?"

"Don't everybody?"

They were silent for a few moments, listening to a distant music.

"Baap?"

God what a beautiful sound that makes when she says it.

"Huhnnn?"

"The other night when I said…no big thing, I didn't really mean—no big thing."

He pulled her into his arms and squeezed her gently.

"I know you didn't mean it, baby. I know you didn't."

* * * * *

He had designated Thursday as letter-writing day and started in at 8:15 A.M.

"Chester L. Simmons, my brother, my brother, my brother…, your letter from the Romanian joint was asskicker."

He carefully studied Chester's envelope to make certain he was spelling Romania correctly.

"Romania don't even sound real to me; it sounds like one of those old funky comic countries that you see on late night TV, where all the people are in uniforms and singin' 'n shit."

He paused, completely blank. What the hell do you say to a brother in jail in Romania? Where in the fuck is this place anyway? Something seemed to unlock after the first stuttering page, like he had stepped through a door and all the right words were waiting for him.

"I know that my Africa is different from your Africa, from what you told me. I didn't meet no kings and queens, but I did meet a beautiful young sister of Cocrobity who was the Ampoty of Ohenna or something like that. I think we would've really hit it off if it hadn't been for her momma. It's been a trip on the lady side, Chester, a real trip. I think I've seen as many beautiful black women in the last month to last me a lifetime.

"Yeah, I hooked up with a couple and I may have HIV from one of them, but I'm goin' to check myself out as soon as we land. I never knew that African women was so fresh, you know what I mean? But hey, you told me about that, you told me how I could get some leg when I couldn't get no food. Remember?

"Talking about food, OK? I don't feel too into Ghana food. Seems like most of the shit is put in a bowl with this fufu and you scoop it out with your right hand. I kind of dug omo tuo. It's got a lot of them down-home flavors in it. They eat a lot of white bread here too, big chunks of it. The smoked fish looks ugly as hell but it ain't too bad with a cold brew. So much for food.

"Except for Cocrobity I really didn't get around a whole lot. Accra is cool, in places, but I don't think I would want to live in Accra. With these open drains I could just see me running down the street and breaking my leg. Somebody ought to do something about the drains.

"Let me tell you something. Yeah, it can do things on your head to realize yourself in a black country run by black people. Like you used (but they have a lot of foreigners here too) to say "travel is broadening."

"Check this out; I went to a reception at the American

ambassador's pad. They was bringing in a new man and they invited Fred and Helene, which wasn't here, so I went instead. I was clean as a broke dick dog—African outfit, eggshell blue with silver pin-stripes. Lots of phoney bull-shit talk, lots of phoney-ass types. You know what I mean. But the thang was that I was on the scene, me, Clyde Johnson from the 'hood.

"I think I must of freaked a few people out. It was kind of nice in a way, like hey I had never been to the ambas-sador's pad at home, OK? Lots of different types of peo-ple. Europeans from Europe, Chinese, Japanese, English people, even Koreans."

He paused to stare at the word he'd written— "Koreans"—and flashed on the painful experiences he and his people were having with this particular group of peo-ple in South Central Los Angeles.

"The Koreans here don't seem like the ones we know; they seem more like Chinese. Flash! No drugs. Yeah, ain't that a trip? No drugs. Don't get me wrong; there is some herb you know, but no rocks, no heroin or ice that I could spot. I know it's some drugs here, but it ain't like the states, OK?"

He carefully placed the ballpoint on the table beside his writing pad and flexed his right hand a few times. Writing was hard work, and he hadn't done a lot of it in his time. He glanced at the little quarter clock—10:12 A.M. *Damn I been writing for two fuckin' hours.* He picked the pen up for a few more paragraphs, but racism triggered another whole page.

"What do you feel when you don't feel like some white boy is goin' to pull the rug out from under your feet? You feel better, that's what. You know, I was here about a week before I realized something. I realized that I hadn't saw a squad car, I hadn't seen nobody get jacked up, and I had only seen maybe ten white people. For the first time in my young life I was not feeling like somebody white was goin' to be fuckin with me.

"Lemme tell you a story. There was this woman selling fried yams at the corner, OK? And I bought some and she tried to cheat me. At first I had this weird feeling, you know, like hey, why would she try to cheat me? I couldn't say 'cause she's different from me, the thang is that I'm a rich Americano and 'cause I got mo' money she's goin' to try to cheat.

"I tripped on that—me a rich Americano! But like, hey, to her I am. It made me think about how po' I used to be in the states 'til I got my thang together. No, Chester, my brother, I'm not doin' that any mo', I give it up. I took your advice and decided it was wrong. I don't want to go into all the steamy details but you know what I mean. I took the money and run.

"That's what took me here. I told my Uncle and Aunt I was goin' to journalism when I return. Think I could be a journalism writer. Hey, I could be anything I want, OK? I went to the Motherland, didn't I?

"I'm goin' back tomorrow, Friday. Write and let me know what you need. The address for my Uncle is my address. I'll be moving from them when I get back, but that's it for now.

"Chester, be cool, later, Bop from the Bricks."

* * * * *

No television worth talking about, a bunch of funny named newspapers, nothing he could really focus on. It was all gin and licentious behavior.

"Bop, you must not think badly of me; I do not come to every man who calls me."

"I know you don't, Patience baby, I know you don't."
There, in that adobe room with the tin-can roof, listening
to the rain and minutes later, the sensual croaking of frogs.
They made love silently, slowly. Periodically, unexpected-
ly, she would gently pull his dick out of her pussy, swab
her pussy with a powdered rag, and re-chart the motions.
He was stunned the first time she did it.

"Uhh, Patience, what's happenin'?"

"Beg you pardon?"

"That's OK, forget it."

One rainy night, after they had lusted each other to sleep,
he eased out of her slave cabin ("boys quarters"), leaving
ten thousand cedis in her limp fist.

"Why, Gbop? Why?"

"'Cause I want to, that's why." *What the hell was ten
thousand cedis, about fifteen dollars or something?*

Elena Boateng didn't need money; she needed sex and
she addressed him to her urge.

"Bap, we should make love more often."

"Huh?"

"Well, you're leaving and then who will I have to make
love with?"

Damn girl, what're you, a nympho or something?

"I hear you, baby, I hear you."

The ceiling fans took him off completely, drenched him
in softly swirling dreams, never nightmares, always dreams.
One soft drenched night, he stared at the ceiling fan until
he became hypnotized or the dreams came. He couldn't tell
one from the other. Midnight in Accra, the helicopters floating above his head made him think of crazy bees. Where
are the police? Where is Uncle David and Aunt Lu?
Yeahhh, there they are, floating above the helicopter,
munching on fried chicken.

Color television made everything seem like funny papers,

the funny papers, the Watts Riots of 1992. He settled back into his feathery chair, sipping Beck's and staring at the funny papers. Color television made everything seem like funnies. The liquor store on the northwest corner of the intersection was being looted. It looked funny on color TV.

Torrance, California. The brilliant sunshine flooded his dream, cast shadows on different places in his mind…. The low stand of mint next to the cactus was a deep green (he had dried some and mixed it with his marijuana a few times), the figs were ripe, the tangerines and oranges were sweetening on the trees. It was a sunny day.

The dinner popped up like a playing card. He was sitting there (was it New Mexico or Mescalero, Mexico?) with six Native American men, eating small, delicately filigreed pancakes. The pancakes were good, but that wasn't the spice of the dream; the spice was the pancake syrup. There was something about the syrup that got him high with each bite.

"Hey, y'all what is this?"

"This is Indian food, shut up 'n eat."

"Twenty-one years old and you ain't done shit with your life but fuck it up…."

"Dave, don't talk to the boy like that, he…."

"It's OK, Aunt Lu; he's right. I need to hear this. Go 'head, Unc, tell it like it is."

The prop wash from the fan back-flushed a wake of warm air over his body, made him shiver deliciously.

"Bop, couple thangs you got to understand. Most people are just milling around like sheep, waiting for someone to lead them somewhere. They're natural followers, most people."

"Awww c'mon, Chester, I don't believe that."

How long was a dream supposed to last?

"Ain't no tellin'; there's a dude in cell block E who says

126

he's been dreaming continuously for the past three years, dreamin' con-tinously...."

Aunt Lulu, Uncle David, dream people. They flicked deserted chicken bones down onto/into his dream, scattering simple logic with barbecue bones.

"If you want to get somewhere or do something, the first thing you have to do is git up off your ass and move!"

The smell of food invaded his dream. "Eat Succotash." Catfish dinners. Chester L. Simmons and his nutritional lectures.

"Now just look at these idiots, Bop; they're pumping iron like it's going outta style. Look at BoBo over there, got muscles between his thumbs and forefingers, but he'll probably drop dead from a heart attack, eating all the grease he eats. I've seen the fool smear lard on white bread."

"Chester, what's this big thing you got with food, man? A hamburger is a fuckin' hamburger!"

"That's what you think, youngblood; pull some of that ghetto snot out of your ears 'n listen up. I got a little-brother-place in my heart for you 'cause I don't really think you're dumb as the rest of these funky chumps."

"What's that mean?"

"It means that I don't think you want to spend most of your life in the slams."

"Like you?"

"Yeahhh, be cruel, youngblood, if you wanna be, yeahhh, like me."

"Sorry, man, I didn't mean...."

"Hey, ain't no thang."

"OK, go 'head, rap to me."

Daily, with practically nothing to do but talk and pump a little iron, Chester rapped/lectured and Bop began to listen.

"Most of the brothers and the Mexicans up in here is

half crazy from the shit they've been loading their systems up with for years. I don't feel qualified to talk too much about our Latino friends, but I *know* what we been eatin' since 1619 is fuuuucccked up."

The prop wash sweltered, back spun, crystallized....

Chester L. Simmons, ex-con man, ex-pimp, ex-ex-ex, managed to convince Clyde Johnson, aka "Bop Daddy," that there was a racist plot behind the pushing of sugar, grease, drugs, and assorted chemicals into the African-American communities across the United States.

"What's this shit with 'fast foods' in our communities?! It's like we don't have time to sit down 'n eat. Most of us ain't got nothin' but time; we ain't got no jobs to rush to. Isn't that interesting? The white boy is dead on the go, phone in the car, phone on the field, ready to go, but you don't see him grabbing those killer burgers and loading up on junk food.

"We spend the same money he spends, buying synthetic shit that don't do nothing but make you have a cravin'.... Check it out, youngblood. Put enough sugar in your tank and it won't run. You'll *think* it's running, but that's just an illusion.

My mother, my father, all of the sweet people in my life— you dirty rotten son of a bitch! I hate you Chester—I love you Chester—I hate you.... Godammit!

"Everything they push in our communities—Afro-African, Afro-Cuban, Afro-Indo-German, Brazilian, Colombian, you get the point. You got to, it's a dream, OK?

"Everything they push in our communities is sweet. I think it's a clever way to get us to swallow some of the bitterest shit the world has ever known. I had a couple funky chumps try to lay some sweet gin on me. You believe that?"

Why does my head ache the way it does sometimes? It's

not a migraine thing; I checked that out. Why must I creep from place to place? No, the dreams don't seem to bear tall standing; I must lower myself. Chester mastered the dream in three of my minds....

"Hey, I ain't got nothin' against eatin' meat. It's what you're eating in the meat that fucks me up. There's got to be some pretty powerful chemical they're using to blow a damn cow up to edible size in four months. Or is it three?

"And, hey, don't get me wrong, I'm not one of those funky chumps who believes that vegetables don't scream 'n cry when we cut and kill them too. It's just a matter of biology. I'd rather kill a tomato or a carrot, which doesn't have a heart like mine, or a liver, or a dick, than slaughter a cow."

Chester was the man who made him understand that white bread wasn't really wonderful and that he ought to pay the Motherland a visit.

Bop felt himself staggering awake, feeling disoriented. *Am I really in Africa? No, my dream takes place here, my nightmare somewhere else.* That's for Rodney King, Benny Powell, Clarence Chance, La Tasha Harlins, the racist pre-New Year's sweeps through the project to arrest the brothers the racist police *thought* would fire their pistols on New Year's, for flooding South Central EL-A with "crack," for making men lie on the ground (their initiation into manhood-humiliation?), for no jobs, for hopelessness, for the secret promotion of gang warfare between the races (within the races) by the Los Angeles Police Department, a fascist government unto itself, for sheer racism.

The fan ground to a stop, the Ghanaians had had enough. It was time to reflect. Bop laughed out loud....

Wowwwwwwwww....

7

He had come to the conclusion that the way the L.A.P.D. allowed the thing to happen was a set-up. Once the fires die down I'm gonna be in Ghana, West Africa, and when the revenge season comes in, I'm gonna be in Ghana, West Africa.

"What you must understand, Bop, is that most of the funky chumps on most U.S. police departments are regimented cowboys with John Wayne-type mentalities. They may lie about, but they're really trained to see things in black and/or white, and they relish that training, like Dobermans.

"They're not like the lifers who're serving time with us in here. They're hundred-yard-dash men, there for the quick glory. A lot of them think they're in the Marines, that's why they say shit like, 'We're in the front line against crime.'"

It was raining again. He was beginning to like the sound of it, and the chorus of strange frogs that made a sound like croaking trombones.

Patience hipped him to it on his next visit to her quarters. "The frogs sound like frogs. How do they sound in America?"

"You don't hear 'em."

She found it odd that frogs didn't croak in his country

the way they croaked in her country.

He sprawled on her mattress on the stone floor, watching her prepare herself for him. She had taken her "baff."

"Gbop, have you had your baff?"

He had never met a cleaner woman in his life. No matter what hour the tyrant she worked for let her off, she took her "baff."

The tyrant that she called "Papa" was as close to a slave master as he would ever know.

"Patience, what're your hours?"

"I heat water at 4:30 A.M."

"OK, so that's when you begin. What time does your workday end?"

Her blank expression said it all. Papa called her with two buzzes of a buzzer inside her room. She was subject to be called at any time.

He was beginning to love the love-preparation ritual. After the "baff," a self-body massage with various kinds of oils and creams, a scraping of the heels with a shard of glass, a liberal dusting of the underarms, breasts, and crotch with scented powders.

"Patience, what do those beads around your hips mean?"

"All girls have these."

"But what do they mean?"

Hesitant pause…. "Men like to play with them."

She sprawled onto the mattress beside him, fragrant, warm, experienced. Her obvious expertise bothered him a bit. He didn't have a clue as to whether he was "ringing her chimes" or not, but she was certainly ringing him. Their soft foreplay wound into hard lovemaking.

The buzzer sounded twice and she shook him off her body like a dog shaking water off its coat.

"Papa!"

He watched her scurry to pull on a gingham house dress

131

and to knot a kerchief on her head.

"I'm coming," she whispered as she scurried out of the door, leaving him literally quivering with anticipation.

Damn, what kinda shit is this?!

He checked the time in a shard of light. 11:15 P.M. This motherfucker oughta be shot…, calling somebody to do something for him at eleven o'clock at night.

Patience had tried to give him some idea of what her work consisted of and when she did it, but he lost track of the bewildering number of things she did.

Ironing, washing, cooking, cleaning, gardening, shopping, serving Papa. She's serving him now. Bop stood and stared out of the only window in the airless room. The large house, the "Big House," was twenty yards away and loomed over the "boys' quarters" like a threatening cloud.

He stood there with his hands on his hips, silently cursing "Papa" and all that he represented.

"Bop, you got to keep something about Africa in the forefront of your mind, 'specially 'British' Africa. Them funky chumps from that little weird-ass island got over there and got ahold of the brothers' minds in a way that no one has been able to successfully explain to me. I mean, how could three or four little puny, pink-faced, constipated, semi-bi-sexual beaurocrats grab hold of fifteen million minds? I'll be a hundred 'n a day before I understand it.

"Right now, I swear to you, at this very minute, you got some Africans who would rather smell a white man's farts than eat a full meal."

"Awwww c'mon, Chester, you gotta be kiddin'!"

"Read my lips. I kid you not. But it ain't just the Africans who were turned out by the English. It's the same way with them fools on the Ivory Coast, in Senegal, with the French, and down in the Mozambique and Angola with the Portuguese.

"You know something? I once did what I thought was a learned study on the subject. You know, why or how or what put so many of the African psyches into such a receptive mode for Eurocentric domination."

"But they dominated us too, ain't that what you told me?"

"Damn right they did! Or tried their damnest to do it with the whip, the branding iron, the gun. And they failed because we were *not* receptive. Dig what I'm saying? We were *not* receptive. It's one thing to drag a funky chump out of his pad, ship him an ocean and a river away and force him to do what you want him to do. It's a completely different thing for someone to come into your house and start telling you how to run things.

"The English, the French, the Portuguese, the Germans, all of the Europeans have been so successful with the African psyche that a lot of the Africans have only one regret."

"What's that?"

"That they no longer have white asses to kiss. And don't believe that all of the black folks in South Africa are happy about seeing the Afrikaner get his lumps."

"You sho' is cold, Chester."

"I'm telling you the truth, youngblood, as Shango is my witness. You'll see it when you get over there. The British are gone but you'll see African brothers treat each other just the way the white boy treated them. And make no apology about it, they'll just straight up treat the lower man like a piece of shit and keep on stepping."

Yeahhh, right again, Chester. He backed away from the window and lay back on the mattress.

"And how did we manage to wind up being so different, so unreceptive?"

"That's been the subject for another one of my learned studies. My basic theory, supported by three sub-theories, is that the actual enslavement process took us completely into the belly of the beast. Like, you know, we went up through the funky chump's intestines, took side views of his heart and liver, and discovered, yea verily! This is a dirty rotten motherfucker we got here.

"Oh yes, we got a few among us who resent the fact that they ain't fully white. But the majority have been unreceptive. If we hadn't been unreceptive, we'd still be pulling plows through cotton fields right now."

Patience returned an hour and a half later, tired again. "Papa needed to have silver polished for the guests coming tomorrow."

The lovemaking that followed her return bordered on the purely mechanical. They both wanted to get it over and done.

* * * * *

He couldn't really figure out what made him do it, but he felt challenged to learn Ga from listening to the sound of the jokes that the brothers made in the Dew Drop Inn.

"Hey, I could learn the shit if I had somebody to teach me."

"I will teach you."

The quiet guy with the pop-bottle-bottom-sized glasses spoke softly but authoritatively.

Bop bought a notebook and had him over for an hour on Monday and Tuesday. He made an excuse for not being available on Wednesday, and by Thursday the project was permanently tabled.

This shit is harder than Chinese arithmetic.

Life in Osu was infinitely interesting on one level, almost boring on another level. It was interesting to see how people occupied themselves, boring to see them do it. The yam lady spent the day frying and selling sliced yams, the kenkey lady spent hours selling kenkey, the little boys pushed makeshift cars through the rutted road, people washed their clothes and hung them out to dry.

There was a flavor about it he couldn't touch, a kind of satisfaction. He spent a half day wandering through the streets, surreptitiously checking out the full, tart breasts of the young women and the gorgeous hips of the mature ones.

Sisters got some butter on these buns, f'real.

And then back to the Vernon house for a cold gin and midday introspection. *What makes this Africa? The people don't really seem a lot different than they do at home. If it wasn't for the language thang, I could be in Watts. Or the Westside of Chicago. The food is different, the way they eat it is different, but what makes this Africa?*

He fought with himself about questions that he knew he had no answers for. *I shouldn't be asking what makes this Africa, I should be asking why am I here?*

That question took him through two tall glasses of cold, meditative gin.

Well, of course, there was Chester L. Simmons' challenge to him. "Bop, I'd be willing to bet you a half dozen granola bars that you'll be back in here this time next year."

"Bullshit! Chester, by this time next year I'm gonna be in Ghana, West Africa."

"Seeing is believing."

Yeahh, how about this, Chester, my man? I'm here. Yeahhh, I'm here, watching dudes in funky little bars pour some of their drink on the ground and say prayers before pouring the rest of it down their throats.

He sprawled on the living room sofa, nipping his gin, tripping a bit. *I wonder why they do that?*

He trickled a few drops of gin onto the floor beside the sofa and tried to think of something sacred to say. "I am

135

now, I was then, and I will always be a Brick."

He swallowed a gulp of gin in imitation of the akpeteshie drinkers and gagged. *Damn, I don't see how they swallow that shit like that.*

The gin seemed to shroud his mind in a fine mist, making him feel as though he could come to grips with stuff he normally shied away from. *Why would somebody take a knife and cut his baby's face all up like that?* They had to be babies when they got slashed up like that.

He subconsciously frowned, recalling a trio of young faces that he had come across on a side street one afternoon. Three young boys, no older than twelve or thirteen, their faces incised with precise cuts. He couldn't stop himself from staring. *Damn, what chick would want a dude with his face all sliced to ribbons?*

One of the regulars in the Dew Drop Inn informed him, "Oh, these northerners, they do that a lot."

"But why?"

"Ohhh, for different reasons, identification, whatever."

Why not get some ID bracelets or something? Why scar somebody up for life?

He did a little stutter step away from the sofa to refresh his gin glass. Chester was right, Africa is heavy.

"Bop, Bop, Bop, youngblood, Africa is heavvvyyyyy. I mean, heavvvvvyyyyy, like layers and layers and layers of heavy. There will be times when you've pulled back one layer and said to yourself—'Uhhh uhhh, so this is what we got under here huh.'

"But then you'll discover that that's just the top layer for the other top layers. And it's that way about everything—people, plants, animals, you name it. Just when you think you got a grip on something, you discover that it ain't what you thought it was.

"Africa slips in and out of you like that. There will be

times when you'll hate Africa and Africans. Yeahhh, your own people. You'll go 'round asking—'why y'all have to be like that?' But then you'll have moments when the love will come down on you so intensely that tears will come to your eyes.

"I've had all of it and some gray stuff in between."

Bop remounted the sofa, a fresh dollop of gin in his glass. Gestures. The gestures always grabbed him, the way people seemed to be telling all kinds of stories with their hands. He had stood off to the side one day, watching Patience and a neighborhood woman talk, their hands fluttering like butterflies. *If the hands don't say it, I can't imagine what could say it.*

The language of the hands was a lot clearer than the verbal kind. Since his aborted Ga class, he had simply allowed the sounds to run into his ears and back out, without giving too much consideration for their meaning.

Wowwwwww…. Ain't this a trip. I'm surrounded by people who could say from one to the other, "Off him!" and I wouldn't even know that the order had been given.

He was impressed by the quickness of the Ghanaian eye. It only took a moment for him to realize that they were on to him, to his total scene. It startled him when the realization first took hold. It wasn't so much a matter of what he could see, it was a matter of what he could feel.

He had the impulse a half dozen times to turn to someone and say, "I know you've scoped my shit; what do you think?"

There was no need to do that. He could read in their body language that they dug him. There was a way that the waitress dug around in her nose while she waited for him to decide what he wanted to eat, the way the brother talked to him as he scratched his ass and pulled the cotton from his crotch.

How many times had they joked with Skateboard about playing with his stuff? That didn't seem to matter here. Women scratched and groomed their crotches as much as men. It just simply seemed to be the thing to do. Titties, noses, crotches, body functions assumed another dimension.

He thought about it for an hour one afternoon, realizing that he had just walked past a naked woman taking a shower behind a pile of bricks. *Wowwwwwwww.*

Ghana, Africa, was changing him, he could feel that. It wasn't simply the gin and the beer. There was something else happening that made him feel strangely frustrated because he couldn't find the words to describe it. It had something to do with how fluid people lived. There wasn't that separation between art and life that he had always been taught (either consciously or unconsciously) to respect.

Here, as the philosopher-poet Donny Hathaway put it, "Ever thang is Ever-thang."

Why do they stack the oranges like that? Damn, I didn't know ripe oranges were green.

He heard the Muslim call to prayer, nodded his head to the rhumba beat of the church drums down the street, and suspected that he was missing something when the drinkers in the Dew Drop spilled gin on the floor and mumbled prayers.

The knocking on the door seemed far away for a moment. *Who could that be?* He pulled himself into a sitting position on the sofa, took a sip of his drink, and carefully strolled to the door.

"Elena?"

"Well, are you going to let me in?"

"You are welcome."

"Well, are you going to let me in?"

"You are welcome."

"You are drunk."

* * * * *

An hour later they were locked in a deadly sexual struggle…. "You are killing me! You are killing me! You are killing me!"

A few minutes later they keeled over into a sexual slag heap, love-drunk and excited by it. He felt her body pressed against him and felt like crying.

You're killing me? Huh? That's a big joke; I'm the one whose going to die. How could you do it to me, Elena, how could you? Here I come all the way over here to get AIDS.

Dammit!

The Vernons were due in a day or so, and he had nine more days to feel Africa.

"Elena, you 'sleep?"

"Yes please."

* * * * *

The next day he wandered through the rutted streets of Osu, alternately feeling sorry for himself—how the hell should a motherfucker feel with a body fulla AIDS?—and strangely elated. The Vernons were due any moment and he felt he had to stuff himself full of experiences before he would be forced to share his life with them again.

The Children of Osu. The glossy photographs came to life in front of him, to the side, behind him. The little girls un-selfconsciously pulling the crotches of their panties to one side for an innocent pee.

The hop-clap game that the girls played every time they stood in a circle. The little boys who used such ingenuity to create rolling vehicles; Ideal milk cans mounted on straight axle sticks, pulled by lengths of wire. Bottle tops punctured to make four-wheel drives, boys rolling bike rims, old car tires, whatever they could find that would roll.

He couldn't really put his finger on what it was about these children that made them so different, so attractive to him. He had never really paid children much attention; they were always underfoot, a necessary evil.

These were different children. They weren't as loud and rowdy as the little brothers and sisters at home. He had never heard one of them cuss, unless they were doing it in a language he couldn't understand.

They didn't jump up in front of you, challenging you to beat them down, or act out of pocket in any way. They were children and they seemed comfortable with the idea.

He didn't feel the same ease with the brothers his own age. *Wowwwww, these have to be some of the squarest brothers on the planet.*

They were drinkers. He checked them out in the Dew Drop Inn. They came into the place, holding hands (he thought that was odd at first), slugged down four or five tots of gin and brandy, and staggered back out.

He couldn't find a fix for them. They didn't seem to pay the ladies a lot of attention, but it was quite obvious that they did like the ladies.

There was just a gap between himself and them that he felt.

It was like they hadn't done anything or been anywhere or seen anything. He kept a cordial distance.

The woman thing was something else. There was a potential girlfriend for him wherever he paused to do anything; the chick at the post office was always smiling at him. The girl in the kiosk with the big juicy lips winked at him constantly. The schoolgirls in their uniforms, who knew he was an American, dropped their voices whenever he came near.

"Hi you young sisters doin' this beautiful day?"

They giggled and one, the boldest with the best command of English, would answer for the group. "Good afternoon."

Yeahhh, it was all flowing to some kind of conclusion: The funerals blocking off sections of the street while people got tipsy and did quiet little dances by themselves, mostly women, he noticed. The colors, always the colors. The old man in his red and green kente weave, the jet black woman in red and yellow stripes, the purples, shocking pinks, autumn russets, the ivory whites, turquoise, shades in between shades.

And I thought my shit was going to be eye-catchin'....

One evening, after a two-hour session of sippin' the local gin at the Shalizar Bar, he stumbled into a chop bar and pulled up on some banku and fish stew.

Wowwww, this shit is good.

He couldn't really decide if it was good because he was semi-drunk, or whether it tasted better being licked off his fingers, or whether it was just good, period.

Wowwww, this shit is good.

He couldn't really understand kenkey, that tamale-like ball of corn that was wrapped in an oil leaf. They oughta stick some hamburger off into the middle of this shit. He smiled, thinking of what Chester Simmons would've said regarding his thought of having hamburger in the kenkey.

"That's the problem with the world today, Bop, too many hamburgers floating around. We got some funky chumps who would rather have a hamburger than have a woman. Hamburgers, to them, have become cigarettes. Maybe they oughta be called ciggieburgers, to give credit to their addictive qualities. But it's not really the hamburgers, or cig-

141

gieburgers, themselves that cause the real problem; it's the mentality that supports that kind of eating. It begins to intrude on every area—'burgeremotions.'

"You slap some pre-fab, pseudo-meat patty on a grill, singe a puffed-up piece of synthetic nerve endings beside it, a few dashes of salt and pepper, and everybody is ready to bullshit each other. The grilled onions lie to the 'burgeremotions,' the pseudo-bread buns collapse at the thought of a real grain, and when a piece of soap-sudsy cheese is mashed on the whole shebang, we're ready to lie each other to death.

"That's the gist of it; we don't want to go too heavily into what burgerization does to a so-called civilization. It's impossible to truly clone extraordinary ideas, feelings, and emotions. Burgerization tends to make a lot of funky chumps believe that they are really on it because they're doing exactly what the next funk chump is doing, either at a faster or a slower pace. They actually begin to think that they're thinking new thoughts, swimming up new streams. Them burger sessions have completely flattened them out.

"Some of them wander off into really bizarre bags: 'What is an African'—seminars on the subject. Langston Hughes, using Simple, explained what an African in America is. But maybe he didn't go well with the kind of mustard they wanted to popularize, so they didn't listen to him too hard.

"John Coltrane blew on 'em. Duke Ellington, with his elegant ass, God, how I love to see that man glide onstage in front of his instrument…. 'Love you all madly, yes, madly.' He could rap.

"Billie Holiday, Miles, Piz, Bird, musical wizards, no cloning possible. Think of what we would have on our hands if they could've cloned Billie Holidays—Lady Day, or Pres?

"'What is an African?'—seminars on the subject, Oh

well, what the hell. Perseverance might be an African trait. I remember a Chinese sage, back in Mac's day, say to me, 'Chester, I don't see how your people stand for all this shit?' Now, he really didn't know what an African was. I could see that. If he really didn't understand that we don't take no shit, then there wasn't a lot to say to him.

"Yeahhh, perseverance might be considered one of the traits we've demonstrated to the world. I'm sure it comes direct from the Diaspora fax machine.

"What is an African?

"What is a human being? Nawwww, no sense being stingy with praise; you gotta give it to the European; he framed a reference for people of color and we bought into it. It would be hard to imagine a seminar on 'What is a European?' But that's what happens when one funky chump gains the uppers in the media game. He can show up to waste time on nebulous bullshit, like 'What is an African?' while he goes on to perpetuate Superman, Tarzan, and a bunch of other mythological stuff.

"The European unwisely pitted himself against the colored world way back when, because of fear of annihilation and his being down in the gutter trying to defend his image ever since. His defense of his urge to be in control has popularized prejudice and racial tensions. Recognize these two relishes for your burger? Prejudice and racial tensions.

"In short, all of these instant coffee things caused us to do ourselves in, here on this planet. I can just see some funky chumps in the next cosmos, peering through the time warp at us, saying…, 'Wowwwww! Look at how them funky chumps wiped themselves out…. They went for the quarter pounder.'"

* * * * *

143

The Vernons came in midafternoon, dusty, irritable, thirsty. He didn't feel that he knew them.

"Bet you been doin' a lotta fuckin' since we been gone, huh?"

The brother could get pretty gross after a couple Club beers. And the target for most of his gross behavior was his wife. Bop checked the scene out closely: been married longer than he had been alive, done a lot of shit together, and now he was tired of her and she was afraid of losing him because she didn't want to be alone.

The first evening back was a heavy one for Bop. Fred got ripped on three Club beers and began to rag Helene's ass. "Bitch! You can kiss my dooky hole! I don't need you! Fuck you!"

She tried to ride it out, placing a dignified look where her self-esteem used to be.

Bop knew the scene well, had been exposed to it a number of times. The man was schizo-drunk and abusive. The woman was the target and victim of the abuse, and after awhile played into being the target and the victim.

Some women he knew had actually defended their abusers. "Awww, Johnny don't mean no harm when he jumps on me like that; he's just drunk and confused."

Chester Simmons, an acute observer of everybody else's domestic scene, put it in other words:

"Most of these battered women, I don't care if it's physical or verbal, become pawns in the 'victims syndrome.' The victims syndrome is what happens when a victim begins to defend her abuser's 'right' to abuse her. It can get real crazy. Real crazy."

"You niggers is crazy! You niggers is crazy!" Fred's nightly litany, under the influence.

Bop felt good about himself, about his ability to ease past a fucked-up couple and onto his own scene. He found

144

lots to do in the streets. Lobster in chili sauce at the Country Kitchen, this big old African hut that was open on four sides.

Wonder what they do when it rains?

Three-hour taxi drives to the Aburi Gardens. "Take me to Aburi."

Four more days to go. He didn't really know how to feel about leaving. He had the feeling he could've done more, but what more? How much more? What?

He rented a room for a day at the Riviera Hotel to get away from the Vernons' shit. Fred was simply cranky when sober and Helene was petty. "Bop, did you eat the last half of the apple that I was saving?"

"Oh, sorry, Helene, I'll buy you another one."

"Buying another one won't be the same."

Well, what the fuck do you want me to do, asshole? This funk chump has ridden your ass so hard you can't hardly hold your head up and now you need somebody to dump on.

I see what the problem is. He kicked back on the bench in his semi-private hut, beachside, and sipped a cold Guinness. *Damn, what a drag. Here these people are in the midst of all this warmth and love and all they come up with is tension and stress.*

The dark-skinned African girls passing by wouldn't allow him to focus on the negatives too long. Sisters got some butter on them thighs.

He stared at the teenaged girl; she must be thirteen at least, playing splash games with several other younger girls. She didn't have a top to her bikini and her breasts stood up like twin beacons.

She was un-selfconscious, playful, beautiful. He seemed to be the only one paying attention to her. It was tricky to put together. Everybody else on the beach wore something on the top. *Why no bra for her?*

145

Maybe she's a village girl. He had had the experience of being driven through some off-brand little hamlet where the women were working, pounding cassava, washing clothes, or whatever, naked to the waist. He rarely paid it any attention after seeing the sight a few times. It was Ghana. Women nursed their babies on the front porch, men pissed against walls, people ate with their hands.

But why is she the only one not wearing a top? He surreptitiously studied the scene until the braless girl and her giggling friends left the waves. The girl draped a beach towel under her arms and made that full body sarong that fascinated him. But they don't wear no panties under there.

Elena. AIDS. He ordered another Guinness.

America seemed so far away. They didn't have any of the shit here that they had in America. No multi-multiii restaurants. Nothin'.

Bop had never been one to stray too far from the pizza parlor, no matter what Chester had laid on him. "Gotta remember, Bop, pizza fucked Frank Sinatra and Marlon Brando up. It's rumored that it even did Orson Welles in."

Frank Sinatra, Marlon Brando, Orson Welles, Chester Simmons' myth people.

No problem with pizzas here. The closest he had come to one was in one of the Lebanese (damn, the Lebanese must be the Koreans of Ghana) stores. It looked like one of their pita bread rounds with something in it.

He stared at his African-time watch. It was still keeping Los Angeles time. *I gotta write Aunt Lu and Uncle David.*

Three days to go. *Shit, they wouldn't get it till I was back home for days. Back home.*

He slumped over his beer. Back home. The Bricks, gang banging. *Wowwwwwww.... Is it true that the Bricks and the*

Keymen have a truce? Won't believe it 'til I see it.

Uzis, dope, Justine, midnight sorties into enemy territory, the sudden flare of sparks, chainsaw reactions. He grimaced at the memory of being shot, of having his body beaten on by someone who wanted to kill him.

Babies being shot up.

Negative images bombarded his head for a few minutes. What it means to *not* be a Brick. A Brick—a Brick—a Brick...an Original Brick.

He felt up under his clothes to caress the scars. These jilly-time motherfuckers over here ain't got no idea what a Brick is.

It was time to close down. He recognized the familiar you-are-fucked-up period from his dope fiend salad days.

"Chester, what do you call someone who has a drug habit?"

"You call the funky chump a dope fiend, that's what you call him."

"But, wait a minute! How about all the latest things that talk about addictive personalities 'n shit like that?"

"Lissen to me close, youngblood; I'm not going to xerox this. A funky chump who is into drugs is a dope fiend. You know what a dope fiend is? I was a dope fiend's dope fiend."

"You?"

"Yes, lawdy Bloody Jesus, I was a dope fiend. I would do anything on Planet Earth for some heroin. You understand what I'm sayin'? I would steal my grandmomma's false teeth, pawn my daddy's railroad watch, lie to my momma, take my sister's rent money. Anything! I hate when they started using 'addict' and put 'fiend' aside. A funky chump who is into serious drugs is a fuckin' Dope Fiend. Fiend, as in *Fiend*!"

Yeahhh, Chester, I hear you.

Bop rang up the screen on his dope fiend salad days. Mornings with a joint and paregoric, a little Ol' English 800 if he had some left over from the night before. A fractured skull. An ankle fractured by a baseball bat. Penal institutions ("facilities") for close to twelve years. Being shot. Ex-drug addict (fiend) pusher.

It was time to stroll the beach. *Twenty-one years old, and I feel like I'm fifty-one. That's one of the things being a Brick will do for you, age you fast.*

Africa. Ghana.

He staggered a few steps, loaded on Guinness and heavy vibes. Where were the warriors, kings, queens, royalty that Chester had programmed him for. He curled his mouth down at the corners.

Just an ordinary run-of-the-mill bunch of black people fuckin' around on the beach. Well, maybe the girl who was runnin' around with no bra was a queen, or a princess, or whatever. But who else?

"Bop, lemme tell you something. Most of these funky chumps in this joint might be the descendants of warriors, kings, queens, royalty. Take a look at BoBo over there. You don't get faces like that unless your genetic bag has been pretty much left uncontaminated. And Waadee, check him out. Now tell me that brother ain't Samburo or Maasai and I'll kiss you on both cheeks in the iron yard."

No, Chester, you got that one wrong. All the dudes you were talking about are them; they're taxi drivers, lawyers, doctors, hustlers, scrub men, students, con-men, video exploitationers, toilet entrepreneurs, serious members of the International School for Children. Now.

He pulled out a palm-sized calculator and made a few swift calculations.

"OK…, there's no need for any suspicion of anything

good happening. Let's be on the alert. Jones! Take the first watch."

What is this crazy shit going through my head? What am I calculating?

He plopped down on a mound of sand with a drunk-silly smile on his face. *Wohhhh, I'm fugged up.*

8

He stared up at the ceiling. A spider was darting back and forth. Fred and Helene were growling at each other in the kitchen. What a fucked-up couple. He's mean and drunk and she's sneaky and greedy. "Bop, I noticed that you cracked a glass while we were gone. You'll have to pay for it."

The spider started down toward him on a single strand. Bop stared, too lazy to do anything about the descending insect.

Damn, wish I had a joint. Or a cold beer. Wonder what time it is? Looks like it's about noon. He parted the curtains and blinked as the sun blasted him in the eyes. Could be noon, could be nine o'clock. The sun seemed to pop up with the same intensity every day. It was hot.

Today is Wednesday, tomorrow is Thursday, through Friday and then I'm outta here. He slowly, carefully sat up on the side of the bed. *Yeahhh, a cold brew, that would straighten me out.* He draped himself in a towel, took his toothbrush, and went to brush his teeth and shower. The yang-yang from the kitchen continued.

He dressed and eased out of the front door. There was no need to inform the arguing couple that he was going to stroll down to the local joint for a cold one.

The worst part of it might be Fred's insisting on joining

him. They had tripped to the local joint once, and Bop made a secret vow that he would never do it again. The locals called Fred "Unca Fred" and swarmed around him. Bop couldn't figure it out. The drunker he got, the more abusive he got and the more they seemed to dig it. After awhile he began to pick up a subtle vibe.

He's kind of a fool to them. They like to hear him cuss and insult people. He's like a fool to them. Bop felt vaguely embarrassed to be out with a gray-haired elder who acted like a fool.

He checked out the African brothers Fred's age. They came in, polished off a few tots, had a little lively conversation, and got back on the track. Fred acted like a fool. He insulted people—"You ain't shit!" He blustered, he threw tantrums, he provoked, got drunker.

"Uhhh, Fred, let's git on back to the pad."

"You git on back to the pad; don't try to tell me what to do. You get me?! You don't try to tell me how to live my fuckin' life. OK?!"

The Shalizar was dim and cool; the lazy fan in the ceiling stirred a few flies around. A quartet of old friends sat at the bar, drinking gin and brandy, exchanging thoughts about the state of the state.

"Taen yowr tang?!

"Mi ya joba."

"Ahhh, that's good, very good. Your Ga is coming."

Bop perked up a bit. The owner of the Shalizar, an attractive, dark-brown-skinned woman with a slight beer belly had spoken to him in Ga—"How is it?"—and he had answered, "I'm fine," without giving it any thought.

Damn, I bet if I stayed over here a while I could speak this shit.

"Your beer cold?"

"Always cold."

"Lemme have a Club."

He sat at a corner table against the window, offering him a perfect picture of the outdoor tap in the vacant lot next to the bar.

The sight of the frosted beer bottle made him thirsty.

"Uhh, what's your name?"

"I am called Betty."

"Thanks, Betty. I needed this. Uhhh, what time is it?"

She studied her watch for a few beats.

"It is 11:18."

"Thanks."

He resisted the urge to laugh. This wasn't the first time he had asked Ghanaians the time and watched them "study" their watches. Maybe they had to wait for the little hand to swing around or something. They studied their watches like something serious was happening, but everybody is always late.

He settled back after a long pull on his beer. *Yeahhh, that's that I needed.* The cool, cave-like atmosphere and low-keyed atmosphere lulled him into an introspective state.

Wonder what's happening in the 'hood with the Bricks? The beer canceled out the gong in the front part of his head. *Damn, wish I had a joint. Oh well....*

He stared through the wood-slatted window at the little girl flushing water into a large bucket at the tap. How old was she, eight, ten maybe? She leaned against the brick wall next to the tap, casually scratching her crotch as the bucket filled.

Beautiful girl-woman. Ten years old and she's doing a woman's work already. A short, natural haircut, doe eyes, a slender body in a see-through cotton dress, no shoes.

He leaned forward involuntarily, vicariously helping her mount the bucket full of water on her head. *Damn. That*

152

must weigh fifty pounds. A whole bucket full of water.

It wasn't the first time he had felt amazed to see someone put something on their heads that looked impossible
for a human being to carry. His all-time favorite memory
of head-carrying was the two middle-aged women crossing
a busy street with flower pots filled with six-foot-tall plants.

*I don't see how they can carry shit that heavy on their
heads. And the babies on the back. What keeps them from
sliding off? I'll have to ask Elena about that.*

Elena Boateng. He gulped a half glass of his beer. *I guess
my dick will be half rotted off by the time I get back home.*
He felt instantly depressed for a moment. *I had to come all
the way over here to catch AIDS. Bet people will be thinking I'm gay or something when this stuff starts showing.*

Midway through his second bottle of beer his mood
changed. *I can't believe I got AIDS, not from a chick like
Elena; she's too clean to have AIDS, not the way she show-
ers 'n shit all the time.*

The quartet of women gathered around the tap drew his
attention. For the umpteenth time he asked himself: *Why
do these sisters straighten their hair?*

Three of the women had straightened hair and were in
obvious need of "touch-ups." Their hair, reddened at the
ends by chemicals, stood out from their heads like spikes.
The fourth woman had her hair done in a fashion he called
"small snakes."

The "small snakes" hair arrangement pleased him. It
made the African woman look like an African woman. The
women with the straightened hair (in this heat!) looked
slightly crazy to him.

"Bop, remember this. When you get to Africa, I think
you'll see cultural imperialism in its rawest form."

"Chester, break it down…. I don't know what the fuck
cultural im-perealism is."

153

"It's when one funky chump decides to push another chump's stuff off to the side and say, 'Look! This is the stuff you're supposed to admire and appreciate. OK? Not that stuff you've been attached to all your life.' The English have done it on a level in Africa that you wouldn't believe. Oh, yeah, they did it in India and some other places too.

"But those places don't concern us as much as Africa. In imitation of the little pink-faced god that they adopted, you'll find Africans having hot tea at two P.M., wearing suits and ties in hundred-degree humidity, giving their children 'English educations,' freaking out to try to get to England, they call it the 'United Kingdom.' But I think the worst thing of all is what they did to the African woman aesthetically."

"Look, Chester, if you gon' talk to me, use some words I can understand."

"Sorry, Bop, I forgot.... you're just a poor, ignunt Brick."

"Awwww c'mon, Chester! You sho' is cold."

"What word did I use that you didn't comprehend, uhh, under-stand?"

"Aesthetic."

"Aesthetically. OK, let's simplify it for your sake and call it 'a standard of beauty,' OK?"

"Cool."

"Starting at the top. The English convinced the African woman that she should make a mockery out of herself by frying, frosting, and ironing her hair. I don't know what kind of PR they use to pull that one off. I mean, when you see some of these sisters two days after the chemicals have faded, it's like looking at somebody with a fright wig on.

"I don't know why they left the men alone on this score. I think they were saving the wool suit with the vest for him. Now you got her in a fright wig and she's trying to bleach her face."

"Git outta here!"

"I bullshit thee not, young Brick. They have some stuff that they lighten their skins with. I'm telling you! The cultural imperialism takes all forms. They'll take an African woman out of her own beautiful clothes and stick her into some crap that makes her look like a European scarecrow. They've convinced them to give their children little blonde dolls for Christmas.

"They've given them 'Christmas,' complete with the reindeer and Sanny Klaus and the whole avocado. We don't want to get into the white Jesus they've given these people...."

"Let's get back to the women."

"Oh, sorry 'bout that. I was about to go on a crusade for a minute. What can I say? They managed to go down into Africa, I'm talking about Ghana specifically, and convince these African women that they're ugly. They're telling them, with hardcore-porno advertising, the movies, magazines, name it, that the only way you can look beautiful is to look like us.

"The fuckin' irony of it is this: at the same time they're trying to wipe the African woman out, the European women are grabbing hold of the African thang as hard as they can. Last thing I read about it was that some European models were having fat injected in their lips to make them bigger and fuller like African women. I don't have to tell you about the suntan syndrome and white women in France doing dances from Senegal.

"It gets crazier and crazier, the more you think about it. They'll push some ol' dull-ass style onto the sister and snatch and grab at her jungle patterns and all that rich color like freaks. And it looks like it's gonna be that way for awhile, before the sisters come back to theyselves. But it'll take years. I see them going through a lot of the madness

155

we went through thirty, forty years ago. Before your time. B.B., before Bop.

"I'm sure a lot of the women would deny it, of course, but what is straightening your naturally kinky hair and dying your natural dark skin? It's symbols of self hatred. We went through that. The sad thing about many of our sisters and brothers is that they don't pay us enough attention. There's a lot we could teach them about how Eurocentric systems corrupt and distort.

"But many of them don't want to hear that. They want to try to pretend that we are not Africans and that our Diaspora never happened. Don't worry, my boy, you'll find enough madness in Ghana to keep your ass occupied all day long."

Bop signaled for another beer. He remembered to hold his hand palm down and imitate someone scratching the air instead of beckoning with his fingers, palm up.

The fright-wigged women and the "small snakes" were replaced by a couple of older women. They were dressed more or less in traditional skirts, except that one had on a T-shirt with the legend, "I am covered with the blood of Jesus."

They stood at the tap, gesturing, obviously enjoying each other's company. They wore scarves on their heads, covering any evidence of "cultural imperialism."

Men strolled into the bar, giving him that half-assed salute that he had learned to imitate. They made him think of the English comedian Benny Hill when he did his imitations of the English Army sergeants.

Two more days. The thought depressed him. *What the hell is the matter with me? I'm going back home. Back home.*

Back home to Uncle David and Aunt Lu? *Nawww, I've already leeched on them as much I can stand it. Maybe as*

156

much as they can stand it too.

Life suddenly seemed complicated to Bop. It was no longer a point of who are you going to stay with, but where are you going to live?

Here I am, twenty-one years old and I ain't never had a place of my own. I either been in jail or living with somebody. It's time for me to get out there. Maybe I could hook up with Justine. The thought of where she was, of the thing that she was into made him feel low, murderous, evil.

Idiot bitch! Why would she have to suck on the pipe? 'Cause You Gave IT TO HER, Pal.... He could feel the old arguments and counter arguments rising up. Crack everywhere; if she didn't get it from me she would've gotten it from somebody else.

"Betty, what time is it?"

Once again the owner held her watch up to study its time.

"It is two o'clock."

"Thanks."

Two o'clock, time for some food. Damn them fools biting each other in the ass at the pad. I think I'll trip to the Kitchen.

* * * * *

The Country Kitchen. A nice buzz in the afternoon.

"Lemme have a cold Club beer and I'll order in a few minutes. OK?"

He liked the Country Kitchen, this huge, African-hut designed restaurant. It was 2:20 P.M. and time to style and profile. The tables were filling up. People came to do serious eating in the Country Kitchen. They had a fine choice of traditional Ghanaian food or Chinese influenced dishes. The Chinese food wasn't the Chinese food of California, but it came close enough.

157

Wonder what would happen if I ordered a burrito?

It was fun for him to trip around by himself; it gave him a chance to filter stuff without having to explain what he was feeling or seeing.

"Would you like to order now?"

"Uhh, yes, lemme have this lobster in chili sauce."

Two thousand cedis, shit; I oughta order two of these bad boys....

"Rice or chips?"

"Chips?"

"Yes, chips."

"What's chips?"

"Potato."

"Yeah, chips, I'll have chips."

He studied the waitress' rhythmic walk away from him. *Mannn, they sho' got some fine sisters in Ghana, straightened hair or not.*

He sipped his beer, feeling grand, on top of it, looked around slyly at the people in the Kitchen. The nut-colored woman with the Raster styled hair held his attention for five whole minutes. Beautiful woman. High cheekbones, lush mouth, gorgeous body; he could see it all at the table. She was alone, eating fufu with goat meat in light soup.

He used his beer glass as a cover, hoisting it and checking her out over the edge. Elegant woman, about thirty-five, probably rich, judging from her clothes 'n shit. Fascinated, he watched her hand dip into the soup, pinch off dabs of fufu, swallow it, grab hold of a piece of goat, and tear a chunk of meat from the bone.

He had never seen anything so elegant in his life. How in the fuck can you dig down into a bowl of soup with your bare hand, pull out a piece of this dough and goat meat, and eat it, looking like a queen.

Bop's second glass of beer almost drove him over to the

elegant lady's table, but some unidentified element held him in check.

Better not make a fool outta myself....

Ten minutes later she had washed her manicured fingers, paid her bill, and departed. Her table was immediately occupied by a couple of potbellied young men in striped shirts and ties.

Must be bank clerks out for dinner.

He tented his fingers under his chin, trying to look debonair. *Wowwww....*

Bop casually looked in the opposite direction before turning his eyes back to the gay couple two tables to his left. *Wowwwww....* They weren't the casually dressed macho guys of Venice Beach or the cool homosexuals of San Francisco. These were the flaming swishes of his prison days; "Bernice" and "Joan." Or "Francine" and "Rosie." They looked like throwbacks and acted like it.

African, Ghanaian gays. Wowwww....

They were so old-fashioned they were trying to act like women. They were in lavender scarves, pastel shirts, high-heeled sandals, perfumed (he liked the scent), and speaking English in high tones.

"So, I just told her, 'You are *annoying* me!'"

"And what did she say?"

"She just lowered her face and apologized. What else was there to do? I mean, I was quite *annoyed*."

"Really?"

Bop peeked around at nearby tables for reactions. No one paid them any obvious attention and, after a few minutes of not attracting any attention, their high tones gradually melted into the general hum.

Gays. I never thought about gays in Ghana, or Africa. Wonder what the lesbian scene is like. They must be here. If you got gays you gotta have bulldaggers.

159

"Awww c'mon, Bop, let's stop calling lesbians bulldaggers and homosexuals fags and punks."

"What do you call 'em, Chester?"

"Lesbians are lesbians and homosexuals are gays. That's the name that they've generally agreed on. People don't call us Negroes any more because most of us have agreed that we are African Americans.

"Let's cool it on the homophobic stuff; it's uncouth."

"Homo-what?"

"Anti-gay talk. Remember, it's just a different form of sex life. That's all."

"Pardon me, may we share your table? The rest of them seem to the filled."

"Yeahh, sure…." Bop felt suddenly wrenched from his sightseeing to deal with the couple standing beside him. He gestured for them to sit down.

"Thank you," they murmured.

The woman was a European and the man was Ghanaian. The three of them sat awkwardly for a couple of minutes. The man broke the ice. "Thank you for sharing your table; the Country Kitchen is becoming more popular all the time."

"Yeah, looks like it."

"I am Paul Mensah and this is my wife, Phyliss."

"Howdyu do?"

They shook hands. The woman was English; he could tell from the clipped sound of her words. English, a strong chin, feathery hair, a prominent nose, penetrating eyes. She made him feel uncomfortable. He didn't have any particular attitudes about mixed couples, but he felt puzzled by African men with white women in Africa.

I don't think I could do it, not with all the sisters tripping around here. I don't know.

"Been here long?" Phyliss Mensah spoke in a very clear, softly accented voice.

"Oh, about forty-five minutes now."

The Mensahs laughed, thinking he was being deliberately funny.

"Oh yes, service can be outrageously slow here at times." He shared the laugh. They were nice people. He relaxed.

"You mean here, in Ghana?"

"Yes, in Ghana. Unless you've been here in this restaurant longer than you've been in Ghana." Yeah, they were nice people, straight up.

"Naww, I ain't been here long. Matter of fact, I'll be going back Saturday."

"You're American?"

Bop felt like laughing. *What the fuck else could I be?*

"Yeah, I'm American."

The waitress blindsided him with lobster in chili sauce and rice.

"Uhh, miss, I ordered chips, remember?"

The waitress allowed a sign of annoyance to curl the corners of her mouth down. What the hell, you've got rice; eat it.

Paul Mensah caught the expression and lit into the waitress in Ga. Bop was surprised to recognize the "kp" and "gb" sounds. The waitress cast her eyes down apologetically and hurried away with his plate.

"Sorry, Mr...?"

"Just call me Bop."

"Sorry, Bop. It seems that some of these people don't pay any attention to what you ask for. You must make them sit up."

Make them sit up. Hell, that's one way to put it.

"She still ain't took you guys order yet." The beer was tangling his tongue a bit.

"Oh, she will," Phyliss added. "Paul knows how to get them hopping."

161

Five minutes later, Bop was eating lobster in chili sauce with chips. Fifteen minutes later, the Mensahs were eating roasted chicken and shrimp fried rice. They were curious about him.

"So you decided to come on your own, you didn't come with a group?"

"Naw, I couldn't see myself being led around by some man with a bullhorn in his mouth. You know what I mean?"

"I quite understand."

"What do you do, Bop, in the states, that is?"

Bop stared at Paul Mensah's mouth for a minute, trying to figure out what to say. *I don't do shit. I used to sell drugs when I was a Brick.*

"I work with youth. I'm a gang counselor."

They literally bubbled over each other trying to ask him about his work. "Oh my! That sounds fascinating. It must be quite adventurous."

"You better believe me, lady.... You could get killed on the job."

"And you're so young. What took you into this line of work?"

Bop was enjoying himself. His belly was full of lobster in chili sauce with chips and his beer high had leveled out. "Hard to say, Paul. It's been more like a callin' than anything else."

"Calling?"

"Yeahhh, you know like they say.... 'Many are called but few are chosen.'"

"Yes, of course."

"Fascinating, absolutely fascinating."

He was at a peak. It was time to move on. He signaled to the waitress. She made a beeline to their table.

"Well, Paul, Phyliss, I gotta git on. A whole buncha stuff to do; you know how it is."

162

They shook hands again. Paul Mensah handed him his card. "I know you're coming back to Ghana; get in touch."

Paul and Phyliss Mensah, Export-Import, African Art, "I will, I will. Y'all take it easy."

He made a grand stroll-exit. The food had absorbed the beer. Now what?

* * * * *

He strolled from Danquah roundabout on the right side of the road. *Here we are in the middle of town and they don't even have sidewalks.* The stores were owned by the Lebanese and the vegetable stands in between were rented and stocked by the Lebanese. They used Ghanaians as front men. He found out by asking, "You own this vegetable stand?"

"No, this belongs to the white man next door. I work here. You are welcome."

He walked to the end of the business district, which ended at Romonas and crossed the street to walk back to Danquah roundabout on the other side of the street.

Ghana is boring. It's like Watts. No movies, no hip places to go, just a bunch of joints where you can go and drink beer and gin. People selling stuff everywhere—bread, shoes, dish towels, can openers, belts, cassettes, plastic, everything. Life struck him as being too serious.

People walked past him, talking and laughing, but he didn't feel that they were really enjoying themselves. Life was too serious to be enjoyed.

It was almost five o'clock, he could tell from the light-weight traffic jam that was beginning to happen in front of him.

Kwatsons. He wandered into the closest thing he had come to that resembled a supermarket in Osu. Three aisles of odds and ends with a butcher shop at the rear and dishes, glasses, stationery, and some more odds and ends upstairs.

They wouldn't know what to do if they saw a Vons, or a Boys or a K-Mart.

He went upstairs to buy envelopes and strolled back out into the humid, dusty street.

Number One, the all-purpose joint on the corner, facing Danquah Circle. "Lemme have a Club beer."

The beer was cold but he didn't have an urge to drink it. He had had enough beer for the day. He slumped in his seat under the beach umbrella, studying the scene. *Wonder if shit would be different for me if I was a Ghanaian? They don't seem to be bored. Everybody seems to have something to do. People are going from one place to another. I see a baby on every woman's back, so I guess that must take up the slack, if you don't have movies or a TV to watch.*

Wonder what Elena is doing tonight? Ain't this a damned shame? I got a thang going on with a woman and I don't even have her phone number. I don't even know if she has a phone. I don't even know where she lives. Time to go back to the Chamber of Horrors.

* * * * *

Fred was in super form. The morning growl session had been fueled by who knows how many beers, and now he was prowling around the house with a beer glass in his hand, degrading his spouse. "You don't mean a fuckin' thing to me! You understand me?! You ain't shit!"

Helene took note of Bop's entrance with a mean look. "Some woman came here this afternoon looking for you."

"Did she wear glasses?"

"Yes."

164

Elena. *Damn. While I'm lushing it up and down the streets I could've been laying up between them pretty black thighs. Shit!*

Fred barely took notice of his arrival except to pause for a swallow of beer and not in his direction. *Good. Don't include me on your hit list; I don't need it.*

He retreated to his room, stripped to his shorts, and sprawled across the bed. The dreams came easy after the beer (how many did I have today?), the good food, the heat and humidity. It was easy to lock Fred out; he had learned how to do it in jail. There was a button you had to push in your head if you didn't want to hear or be included in everybody's escape plan, the he-said-they-said bullshit, the occasional sadistic guard, the mutterings and snoring of hundreds of people locked up together.

He was on a road with a red stripe painted in the middle of it. The road was walled in on both sides by lush green jungles. He walked toward the horizon on the road, taking note of the fruit that grew on the trees. There were moments when he felt himself floating above the road, but he was following the red stripe, whether on the road or in the air.

Huge birds with pelican beaks swooped back and forth in front of him as he slowly made his way through one hilly stretch of the road. "Keep going, keep going, keep going," they seemed to be saying. "Keep going, keep going." It was a weird bird song.

The road curved and, as he rounded the corner, a gigantic, charcoal-colored woman stood in the center of the road, naked, smiling at him. Charcoal textured, with snow white teeth, short nappy hair, gorgeous breasts and hips, incredibly female. She beckoned to him in the Ghanaian way with the palm down and said, "Ba—Ba, come."

He walked toward her, feeling small, strange, inadequate.

She's too big for me. She must be six feet tall. As he approached her she turned and started walking away from him. He hurried to keep up. Her pace was unhurried but he couldn't reach her side. He managed to match her pace ten strides behind.

Her back was strongly muscled; the indentation between the top of her body and the bottom perfectly molded. *Wowwww.... What is she? 50-22-50 or something?*

He wanted to run up behind her and run his hands along the curve of her buttocks. *I ain't never seen a ass this perfect.* He felt mesmerized by the rhythm of her walk, every lilting step was an invitation to dance, to touch.

Bop could feel himself becoming aroused. *She's too big for me. I'd be like a baby in her arms.* He felt that feeling, but he couldn't push the erotic element to the side.

She turned to smile at him, encouraging him.... "Keep going, keep going, keep going," the birds whispered now.

Suddenly she stopped, turned to him, opened her arms, and spoke for the first time. The voice sounded familiar but he couldn't place it. "Come, give me your love."

He approached her hesitantly, and as he did so, she began to shrink. He was within five yards of her and she was his size.

"Come, give me your love; I need it desperately."

He floated into her arms and they kissed. It was a long, feverish kiss. He felt his mouth being glued to her lips and wanted to pull away, but he couldn't.

And then he opened his eyes in panic and saw that he was kissing Justine, and her face was a network of scratches, scars, termite carvings, decayed, ugly. He screamed and woke up simultaneously.

"Whatcha doin' in there, motherfucker! Jackin' off!?"

Fred was still at it; Helene was still taking it. Bop pulled his bathtowel from the chair beside the bed and scrubbed

166

the sweat from his face and upper body.

What the fuck was that about? How long have I been asleep? He peered through the dim moonlight streaming into the window, at the quartz clock on the bedside table. 7.30 P.M. Well, they say you dream when you just go to sleep or when you're just getting ready to wake up.

The tiny rivulets of sweat from his forehead and armpits continued for a few minutes. He trembled but he couldn't get away from it. *Justine. He had managed to blot her out of his dream-consciousness for days. Justine. Maybe I'm getting malaria again.* He palmed his forehead. Just perspiration, no fever. *Justine.*

He flung the towel across the room and sprawled out with his hands interwoven behind his head. *Why in the fuck should I feel guilty about her? She had her mind about her when she decided to do what she wanted to do. Why should I feel guilty?*

He dabbed at the perspiration rolling off his temples and discovered he was crying. *Oh wowwww.... An Original Brick crying. Wonder what they would say about this?*

The tears simply rolled out of the corners of his eyes for a few minutes, uncontrollably. He felt stupid, crying, because he couldn't really focus on a reason for his tears.

I really fucked that girl up. I'm gon' have to do something for her when I get back.

He remained awake for an hour after Fred finally swore his way to sleep on the living room sofa. "Fuck you, you stinky bitch!"

Releasing Helene to have a nightcap of gin and brandy, and a tortured sleep.

167

9

Helene woke him up with a sour expression on her face. "That woman is here again. Couldn't she wait until people got up before she started visiting? It's only 7.30 A.M. and we didn't get in bed 'til late."

Kiss my motherfuckin' ass, Helene; I don't have to be a genius-psychologist to see where you're coming from. After somebody had ragged my ass the way you got ragged last night, you're looking around for a chance to brush some of that shit off your head.

He ignored Helene's ill-tempered remarks and pulled Elena into his room.

"Hi baby; I'm glad to see you."

"I thought you would be. Put some clothes on; we're going for a ride."

Thursday. One more day 'til kick-off....

"Shit, I didn't know you had a new car."

"There are many things you don't know about me, Bop," she said, sounding mysterious.

"Hey, you got that right, lady."

Funny little car with wood paneling on the doors, looked like somebody had made it by hand. Minor 1000, whatever that was. English.

He was stunned to see the road they were on, how much it resembled the road in his nightmare. *If I see a red stripe*

I'm jumping out of here.

"We're going to Larteh, to my mother's ancestral town. Some people might call it a village, but I think it's a town. And we will visit the shrine of Akonodi to ask Okomfohene Nana Oparebea for her blessings."

He studied her profile. *Damn, this is a fine sister, but she's crazy as a Betsy-bug.*

"We gonna do what?"

"Don't worry. It'll all be painless. And then I thought we could have lunch at Tamara's and spend the night and return in the morning."

"You got it all mapped out, huh?"

"Yes."

She was fun to travel with. She told weird little stories. "There were three men on a bridge; all of them fell into the river and one of them came out of the water without getting his hair wet. Which one was that?"

"Damned if I know."

"The bald one."

"Oh, I see, said the blind man."

They took wayward turns off the main road to stare at mud-walled hamlets. "Our people need better housing, better feed, more medical facilities, a manufacturing capability."

"Sounds like you need a whole bunch of things."

They paused to buy sugar cane, had it cut into edible lengths, and sped off, spitting the residue of the juicy stalks onto the road.

She was a regular. He liked the way she ignored the sap from the cane running down her chin.

"We must get some watermelon; I love watermelon in the countryside."

They found a watermelon stand three miles up the road, purchased slices, and spat seeds as the journey continued.

Ten A.M. The sun and the hum of the motor had lulled them into a quiet place. They passed people on the roadside carrying logs on their heads.

"Elena, did you see that? That woman carrying a tree trunk on her head."

"Oh! That's the way they carry things here."

"I know that, baby, but a tree trunk?!"

The Ghanaian countryside didn't seem receptive to the idea of picnicking. Or lovemaking. The roadsides were dense and hostile-looking to him. It wasn't the first time he had been in the countryside, and once again he asked himself: *Could I live out here, in this?*

"Beautiful, isn't it?"

"Yes, beautiful."

He looked at her thighs through the thin fabric of her dress, the way the muscles rippled as she worked the clutch and the gas pedal. He felt tempted to simply ask her point blank…. Elena, do you have AIDS? Have you had sex with anybody else over the last ten years who may have had AIDS?

She placed her right hand on his left thigh and canceled out all questions.

"I think I'm going to miss you, Bop."

"You better."

* * * * *

Larteh came at the end of a curve in the road. Suddenly, after a gentle winding around a few hills, they were on the main street.

"Larteh is simple. If you're going uphill, you're going into town; if you're going downhill, you're going out of town."

She drove uphill through the clots of people, exchanging greetings and comments with people.

"Looks like you know everybody in town."

"Just about; this is where I spent my earliest years."

They came to the end of the street and she parked in a vacant lot, an imposing house with a stone porch on one side and a church on the other side.

"Well, here we are."

"Well, where are we?"

"This is the home of the chief, my mother's senior brother. He isn't here now; he has a business in London, but my uncle Bobby should be here."

"Your mother's brother is a chief?"

"Yes."

The girl is full of surprises. *A chief.... Wowww. Then she must be a princess or something.*

"Let's sit here for a few minutes."

They occupied seats on the porch, and within minutes a young man came with a pitcher of ice water and two glasses. "You are welcome," he murmured and padded away.

You are welcome. They didn't say, "Welcome," or, "Glad you came," or anything like that. They always said, "You are welcome."

"Elena, why do people always say, 'You are welcome?'"

She looked puzzled for a few beats and pushed her glasses up on her nose in a characteristic gesture.

"You are welcome. That's what that means."

"Thanks, sweet thang; you've just explained the whole thing."

"You are welcome."

She clearly understood his frame of reference and she mocked him for it. You are welcome.

A wild-looking dark-skinned man with bloodshot eyes and an expensive piece of cloth swathing his potbellied body staggered around the corner of the porch.

"Elena!"

"Uncle Bobby!"

And from that point on Bop felt himself in an undertow of liquid Ga for a few minutes. He was beginning to like the flow of the sound. It seemed that people were playing musical mouths with each other. Before she stopped speaking, the other was responding, or maybe, he reasoned, it just seemed to sound that way to his ears.

"Clydee Johnson, this is my Uncle Bobby Adjei Danquah."

They shook hands and did the finger snap and took careful measure of each other. Bop liked Uncle Bobby right off. He liked the way he straightened his cloth on his shoulder and threw lascivious glances at the full-hipped women walking past.

This motherfucker is a player. Elena took note of what he was noticing and telegraphed a shy smile in his direction: Yes, he's all the things he seems to be.

"Elena, have you taken him inside the palace?"

The palace? What the hell is he talking about?

"No, uncle, we were waiting for you."

"Oh!"

He stuck his hand out to Bop like an American politician asking for votes. Elena had to race to keep up.

"I introduced you already, uncle."

"Well, so what? It never hurts to meet good people coming and going. I am called Bobby Adjei Danquah."

"And I am called Clyde Bop Johnson."

The uncle was slightly tipsy but obviously in control of his scene. He herded them through the door, opened another door, and pushed them into a room that was as spacious as an auditorium. Bop estimated it to be as large as a football field, about fifty yards across and a hundred yards from end to end, with plush sofas surrounding the edges.

Damn, this is a palace.

"Sit! Sit! Sit!"

Uncle Bobby was all over the place, ushering them to seats near the door.

"The chief is gone. Official business. Clyde, will you take something?"

"Uh huh."

Bop had learned not to refuse anything. It was always easy to ignore it, once you got it. The important thing was to get it.

Elena settled back on the sofa, looking amused as Clyde Bop Johnson, a Brick, dealt with Uncle Bobby Adjei Danquah's effervescence.

Uncle Bobby clapped his hands twice and the same young man who had brought them water on the porch appeared.

"Bring us the gin!" Uncle Bobby commanded. He turned to Elena and spoke rapidly in Ga. And turned back to Bop. "I told her she should come home more often; Accra is no place for a young woman. Now then, you are here to pay your respects to Nana, eh?"

"Eh? Uhh, yeah, we're here...."

"Good. Ahhh, the gin."

Uncle Bobby gave him the impression of a man in constant motion; he gestured, he rearranged his beautifully woven cloth over his left shoulder, he squirmed, he talked, he drank.

"To the good life," he toasted, holding his tulip-shaped wineglass full of gin up to the light. Bop matched him with his glass; Elena took a timid sip.

Once again, Uncle Bobby turned to her and spoke in Ga. He turned back to Bop for the translation. "I told her to go visit the family house. We will meet her there later."

"Uncle, we are here to see the Okomfohene Nana Oparebea...."

"I know. I know. And you shall meet her this afternoon. A group of African Americans are going to meet with her this afternoon at three o'clock."

"Did you say African Americans?"

Uncle Bobby took a swallow of gin and laughed. "Yes, your people, OK?"

"Yeah, I'd like to see them."

Beefeater, a quart bottle, it shot straight to the top of his head. He was high after a half glass. Uncle Bobby whipped another dollop into his glass.

Elena was smiling at the scene. Uncle Bobby stood up suddenly, pouring the contents of his glass down his throat in the same motion. "Come, Bop. We'll go to meet my friends." Once again he herded them out. Bop felt like a schoolboy.

"Elena, can you find the family house?"

"Yes, uncle, I can find it."

"Good. Go there. We will come to collect you at (Bop noted Uncle Bobby's study of his watch) 2:30 P.M."

"Yes, uncle. Do you want me to drive you to where you're going?"

"No, it isn't far; we'll walk. Walking keeps me fit."

Bop was surprised to notice how meek Elena had become. When her uncle spoke she almost bowed.

"Come with me, Bop."

Bop got the impression no one had refused to do anything Uncle Bobby wanted them to do in a long time. Elena sprinkled her fingers at him, as though to say, "Good luck, pal."

"See you later, Bop."

"Yeah, see you later."

Suddenly he was torn from his lady's side and was trailing in Uncle Bobby's wake. The man didn't walk, he sailed down the street. Bop felt lost, watching Elena drive past them.

Uncle Bobby reached back and clamped his heavy arm around Bop's shoulders.

"We are men. Do you have a thousand cedis?"

* * * * *

Bop began to nag Uncle Bobby at 2:15 P.M. "Uhh, Uncle Bobby, it's 2:15; I think we oughta be picking Elena up, you know, for our meeting with the No Na."

"There's time; cheers! Don't worry."

By 2:15 P.M., Bop felt that he knew every bar in Larteh. Uncle Bobby was well known and obviously an important man. He opened up paths through groups of people by pushing people aside. When he spoke, everyone paid close attention. And he could drink. Bop had to give him that. After the Beefeater at the palace, he had watched him down a Guinness stout in three swallows, share a glass of Club beer in the Zanzibar, drink a double tot of gin (local) in the Sugar Cane Club, and now, at 2:30 P.M., in the place called Mery's Bar, he was sharing a double tot of gin and brandy mixed with a group of men who closely resembled him in age and behavior.

These brothers act like they own the world. It was a new experience to see gray-haired men with potbellies act so boldly. He could only contrast/compare their attitudes with the men their age in L.A., who went around with low profile, seeming to beg with every gesture to be left alone.

How many times had he heard some middle-aged man say, when he was a Brick, "I don't want any trouble." These men weren't concerned about anything like that. They gave orders to younger men and, drunk, with their "togas" drawn up, walked through the streets like lords. He was impressed.

"Uhhh, Uncle Bobby, I don't wanna bug you or any-

175

thing, but remember we promised Elena we'd pick her up. Remember?"

Bop was finally able to persuade him to leave at three P.M., after having spent four thousand cedis. Yeah, the brother could sip well.

Elena didn't seem surprised to see them late and tipsy. "I didn't expect you 'til later."

"But I thought we was s'posed to be at the shrine place at three o'clock."

"Bop, how long have you been in Ghana?"

* * * * *

After quickie introductions to a succession of smiling female faces and limp handshakes, they were once again trailing Uncle Bobby back up the street to the Shrine of Akonodi.

"Elena, who were those women?"

"My mother's sisters, Uncle Bobby's wives...."

"Wives?"

"Yes."

"Which ones were the wives?"

"Christina, Mercy, Grace, and Rosemarie."

"He's got four wives?!"

"He had six; two of them died."

Bop stared at the glittering figure striding up the street in front of them, exchanging greetings and glad-handing colleagues. *Wowwwwww....*

Up the street to a blackboard sign: "African Traditional Religion, Okomfohene Nana Oparebea, Life President of Traditional Psychic and Healing Association of Ghana."

The path veered off to the right, a rock-strewn path that seemed to trickle down to a natural amphitheater. The drums grabbed him halfway down the hill. The drumming sounded like a giant heartbeat to him, with little rattles going on between time.

Uncle Bobby gave him a long, mysterious look as they came off the path onto a paved terrace. Bop felt like he had wandered onto a movie set. Nothing seemed real.

There were three terrace levels, and sheep were being slaughtered on each level. People were busily going back and forth, doing whatever. And flush in the middle of it, against a far wall, a small, dark, wrinkled woman sat on an elaborately carved stool, her head held in her right hand, looking seriously interested and bored at the same time.

Elena whispered into Bop's ear, "That is Okomfohene Nana Oparebea; they say that she was the force behind Nkrumah."

N-krumah N-krumah N-krumah what? Bop drew a blank for a few beats. *Nkrumah? Chester had thrown the name at him half a dozen times.*

"Nkrumah was a visionary dude. He was coming off with stuff about a United States of Africa; you *know* the CIA had to figure out a way to snuff him out."

Everything seemed to be happening at the same time. People were talking to Okomfohene, sheep were being bled, the drummers were drumming, and suddenly it all stopped.

"Where are the brothers and sisters from the states?" Bop whispered to Elena; she relayed the question to her uncle, who pulled an important looking, baldheaded man with dreamy eyes over to one side to repeat the question.

The answer was simple: "They are not here."

Bop had to smile. *Ghanaians could come up with the funniest shit. I can see they ain't here; where are they?*

He decided to table the question and go with the flow. Uncle Bobby and the baldheaded man had their heads together. The baldheaded man turned from his head-to-head conference a couple of times to stare at Bop.

Uncle Bobby gestured for them to come to him and the baldheaded man.

"Would you like to receive Nana's blessings?"

"Huh?"

"Yes, we would," Elena answered for them.

"Did you bring schnapps?" The baldheaded man asked.

"Yes," Elena answered again.

"Come," the baldheaded man said and led them to seats a few yards to the left of the Life President of the Traditional Psychic and Healing Association of Ghana.

Bop's mouth felt dry and, after all the sipping of the afternoon, he felt completely sober. He made an oblique study of the old woman seated on the throne-stool. *She must be older than dirt.*

He had never seen anyone who looked so completely old and wise. He felt a vibe that told him that she knew he was looking at her. Weird feeling. She didn't turn her head and make any effort to have eye-to-eye contact with him, but he knew that she knew he was checking her out.

Bop felt his stomach rolling around. *Damn, I hope I ain't got diarrhea.* And some bright spots danced in front of his eyes. *Oh shit! Malaria....*

"You have the schnapps?" The baldheaded man was standing in front of them.

Elena reached into her purse and pulled out a green bottle labeled "Henkes." Bop felt like he was on the edge of something but couldn't fall off. He was afraid, but he couldn't place a label on what he was afraid of.

What're they going to do to me?

Uncle Bobby was seated two chairs away, chatting with a distinguished looking gray-haired man in a dashiki. Things had a strange blend; they were quite casual, but at the same time he felt something different happening to him.

The baldheaded man suddenly called to him to come and

kneel before the Okomfohene.

"Huh? Who? Me?"

The man called to him again with his hand and one silent word, "Ba." Elena pushed him out of his seat.

The man said some words to the old woman and asked Bop to kneel in front of her. Bop knelt and when he looked into the old woman's eyes he felt like a piece of glass. The old woman stared through him, he could feel that, but as he focused, adjusted his eyes to meet hers, he could see scenes. He saw himself playing in a vacant lot in Chicago. He could see the green paths that bordered Lake Michigan, pleasant scenes of people having picnics, family dinners during holiday times. *Chicago. Shit, I ain't thought about Chicago in a long time.*

The slide suddenly slipped to California. He could see himself driving through the San Bernardino Mountains into Crestline, thirty thousand dollars in a gym bag, Justine sleeping in the back seat.

Justine again. After a January weekend at the Kannas Hotel, leaving Crestline with two inches of fresh mountain snow on the hood of the car, down to three days at the Santa Monica Hotel, snow melting all the way.

"Please, please, return to your seat." The baldheaded man was speaking to him and the old woman was smiling oh so sweetly. He wished that he could remain kneeling in front of her a bit longer.

He returned to his seat beside Elena, unable to speak about what he had just experienced. A couple of minutes later, as he was beginning to sort it out, the baldheaded man stood before him with a shot glass and the bottle of schnapps. He poured a full tot and Bop drank it, remembering to pour the last drop on the ground. *My Dew Drop Inn training.*

A few minutes later the okyeame (the baldheaded man)

was signaling for him and Elena to come and kneel before the Okomfohene again.

Bop was surprised to feel Uncle Bobby kneel behind them. The baldheaded man asked, "And is this your wife?"

Bop made a numb nod, no.

"Are you going to marry this woman?"

It was Uncle Bobby behind them asking the question.

"I don't know," Bop answered as honestly as he felt.

"Where is your life going?" the old woman asked, with the baldheaded man translating.

Bop stared at her and felt like crying....

"You tell me, sister, you tell me...."

The old woman smiled at him, took the green bottle, and poured some of the liquor on the ground in front of their knees and turned her vision back inwards.

The baldheaded man and Uncle Bobby shepherded them back to their seats. Bop felt like he had had some terrible shit mashed out of his soul.

* * * * *

Tamara's. They sat at a choice table in this overpriced hotel restaurant, overlooking the valley that led to Larteh. The food was delicious and overpriced, the beer was too cold and overpriced, but the view into the valley was gorgeous and their vibes were honed to a fine edge.

"Elena, what do you think about this afternoon?"

"I grew up in Larteh, remember?"

"What's that mean?"

"It means that I've been in the Okomfohene's presence many times."

"Oh."

There was so little to say and so much understood in Africa. Bop felt older, more mature. This scene wasn't

180

about uzis, dope, flashy craziness; it was about how deep you could get. Chester had warned him.

"They'll be peeling layers back on your ass in Africa, Bop. I'm not bullshittin' you. You'll come across shit that will have you frowning or smiling for years, if that's where you think you want to go. In Ghana, for example, the West African country with the friendliest, most gracious people on the continent, everybody lies. Why?

"You hear what I'm saying? Everybody lies! I don't even know if they know they're lying or not. It's like a part of the national character. A taxi driver will say, 'I'll collect you at eleven o'clock tomorrow morning.' You may never see him again. You can make a date with a woman for Friday, May whatever, and not see her 'til the following May. People will come up to you and lie when they don't have to lie. 'Oh, you're looking for a flat? My brother will rent you a flat tomorrow.' You may never see that person again. And on and on and on....

"I've never been able to figure out what it is. Maybe it's a reaction to the kind of truth they were forced to come to grips with when the English ran their asses. I don't know. The shit is deep."

Some European tourists had had a few too many beers and were starting to become obnoxious. Bop and Elena exchanged coded looks. It was time to go to bed.

* * * * *

Friday. The car hummed along.
"This your car?"
"Oh no, this is my cousin's car. She loaned it to me."
"Oh."
Sugarcane juice running down her chin, watermelon seeds, Larteh, Uncle Bobby, the Okomfohene Nana

Oparebea, Tamara's, the look into the valley.

"Just..., Elena?"

"Yes?"

The green countryside seemed to promise something if you could stand still long enough for it to curl around you.

"Elena, pull over for a minute; stop the car."

"You have to urinate?"

"No, I have to tell you something."

She slowed down and killed the engine on a track off the road. She turned to him with a blank look on her face. "Yes?"

Ghana was so quiet. No crickets, no birds chirping, no lions roaring....

"Look, I think I love you. OK?"

"OK."

"Well?"

"Well, what?"

"Well, what're we going to do about it?"

Elena shook her head from side to side for a few beats, as though she were trying to ward off a persistent fly. Or a headache.

"I'm not going to do anything. There's nothing I can do. You're boarding a British Airways flight to U.K. tomorrow and from there to Los Angeles. Correct?"

"Yeahh, that's true, but I'm telling you I love you."

He was horrified to see the look of the old woman suddenly appear behind her glasses...when she turned to face him. And fascinated.

"Bop, let me tell you something. I've thought a lot about this. The African woman has been the most loved woman in the world. And the most abandoned. Do you understand what I'm saying?"

Bop looked far off at a distant tree and thought about something to say; nothing registered. He nodded no.

"I can't take you back to the beginning of time or anything like that. Let's start at the fifteenth century."

"The fifteenth century?" She was beginning to sound like Chester.

"Yes. The fifteenth century. The Portuguese came and they fell in love with us, with the African woman."

"Oh yeahh, I see where you comin' from."

"The French fell in love with us, the English, the Dutch, the Germans, the Danes, the Lebanese..., the African Americans, and you've all left us."

Bop stared at Elena's face. No, it wasn't the face of the old woman; it was Elena's face and she was trying to explain something to him.

"Uhhh, so, you say all that to say what?"

"I'm saying all that to say that I don't think it's incredible that you are in love with me, the African woman."

"Wait a minute, what's that mean?"

"Does it mean that you're going to stay here in Ghana with me or go back to where you came from?"

"My visa is up, baby."

"I understand."

She started the car and drove on.

* * * * *

He had to endure Friday night in order to get to Saturday. Fred went into a special brand of narcissistic mysticism that forced him to strip buck naked and roam through the house with a bouquet of burning sage, screaming out Club beer chants.

"Woogie Woogie Boogie Choogies, Chobbbie Woogie...."

Bop lay in bed, amused rather than suffering from the incantations and silliness. *It would do this brother a lot of*

183

good, I think, to take a trip to the Shrine.

Fred finally collapsed at two A.M., and Helene blessed his naked frame with a blanket on the living room sofa. *They don't have anything to do with each other. Maybe that's what the problem is. Maybe they ought to try a little sexin' 'n shit. But who am I to talk? I'm leaving.*

* * * * *

He got up slowly, determined to follow a routine, no matter what. He was beginning to see some value in having a routine. Push-ups. Brush your teeth. Walk over to the soccer field for a little workout, back home for a shower.

The Vernons were early risers, but he really couldn't figure out why they got up so early. Maybe it was to turn the air blue with cigarette smoke and bad vibes. They both smoked and he was reminded one evening, after they had gone through two packs each, of something that Justine had once said: "Kissing a man who smokes is like licking an ashtray."

Justine.

People began to filter in about elevenish. He was pleasantly surprised....

"Thought we'd throw a little beer bash for your ass."

Fred amazed him. He could get completely out of it at night and then stroll around the next day as though nothing had happened. The people wandering in were the ones who had popped in while the Vernons were up north and a few faces he hadn't seen before.

He was surprised to see the fine brown-skinned sister he had clowned with at the embassy. "Hope you make it back; take it easy."

She moved fast, shot quickly, and took no prisoners. Fast sister. Nice gathering. People strolled around with bottles of beer in hand or something harder, paused to chat with him.

"Hope you'll have good things to say about us Ghanaians."

"Oh yeahhh, lots of good things."

He felt like a celebrity. Elena blinded him with her appearance.

"Heyyy, Elena, I'm glad you came. I didn't know if you was gonna see me off at the airport or what."

She looked uncomfortable. "I'm not going to the airport with you; I'm not good at departure scenes. Here, I have a present for you." She took a kente cloth scarf from her purse and draped it around his neck. "This is the real kente. I want you to remember me."

They wedged themselves through what had become a house full of partygoers. Fred was progressing toward drunken hostility. They stood outside the gate beside her car.

"Cousin let you use the ride again, huh?"

"Only to visit you. I have to return it within the hour."

An hour. No time to go anywhere, to do anything. He felt awkward and frustrated. "Can we sit in the car a minute?"

They sat there, watching the women with loaded trays on their heads walk past. Little boys kicking a deflated soccer ball, girls playing the hop-clap game in the cluttered lot across the street.

Saturday in the Osu 'hood. No drive-by shootings, no graffiti on the mud-crusted walls, no screeching cars twisting around corners, no John Wayne policemen, just people hustling to survive.

"Elena, look, I've really had a good time with you, OK?"

"Yes please."

Were those tears running down her cheeks? Wowwww.... What's going on here?

"Heyyy, what's the matter? You OK?"

"Yes, I'm OK."

He patted her hand. What else was there to say?

"Look, I told you I loved you yesterday. I meant that."

"I believe you."

"Yeahh, it's true. I do love you."

"Bap, I love you also, I think."

It was becoming too complicated for him. What now? *I've told her I love her and now she's telling me she loves me too. What now?*

"Elena, look, let's stay in touch, OK? You have to give me an address or something so that I can write you."

She dug into her purse and handed him a card with her name and a post office box number printed on it. "You can write me here."

"OK, I will."

"I must go now."

"Gimme a kiss."

She leaned over and gave him a dry peck on the lips. *Well, what could you expect? You're leaving.* He got out of the car and walked around to the driver's side.

"I'll write you as soon as I can, OK?"

She had taken off her glasses and he could see the tears clearly. *Wowwww....*

"Good-bye, Bap."

He stood there for a few minutes, watching her dodge potholes as she drove away. *Women are so weird. Just when you think you got a handle on them, they fly off in another direction.*

"Bap, I love you also, I think."

Fred was warming up; he could hear his voice snarling higher in a one-man argument with himself. Bop backed away from the gate and began an aimless stroll up the road.

Let me go check Patience out.

* * * * *

Patience was working. She was hauling buckets of water to the second floor; she was cleaning, scrubbing, washing, ironing, working. She stopped when she saw him in the back area, on the bench between the big house and the boys' quarters.

"Have you chopped?"

"Yeah, I had a sandwich about an hour ago."

She sat beside him on the bench, looking tired but cool. "They are having a party for you but you are here. Why?"

"How did you know they were having a party for me?"

"This is Osu."

He felt the temptation to ask her if she knew about his departure scene with Elena. Yes, of course, she knew. "This is Osu."

For the second time in less than an hour he felt ill-at-ease, awkward. *Should I tell Patience that I love her too? Nawww, she doesn't need that.* He looked down at her hands folded in her lap.

Short, stubby fingers, callused. Who was it that said people with stubby fingers were artistic? Somebody.

"Papa is not about."

"Not about what?"

"He has gone out."

"Oh." *And left you to work like a dog 'til he gets back. And then he's gonna really make you work.*

A rooster crowed in the next yard. The sound of children screaming and playing broke the silence. She took his hand and led him into the boys' quarters.

Two hours later, after carefully making love to each other, after a brief sexual catnap and a long conversation....

"Patience, I think I may come back to Ghana."

"You are welcome."

He strolled through the streets, tripping on familiar scenes. A pause for a cold beer in the Dew Drop..., a double tot of gin in the Shalizar.

"So, you're going back to America this evening?"

"Damn, Betty, how did you know?"

"This is Osu."

He found himself strolling through the tree-shaded lanes in the Osu Cemetery, one of his favorite rest spots. He sat on one of the stone slabs—"Here lies Malcolm Quartey, man for all seasons—1935–1989."

Here sits Clyde Bop Johnson, twenty-five years old, an original Brick, been shot, beaten, fractured, fucked with, still alive.

He leaned back and rested his elbows on the cool slab. *Accra, Ghana, West Africa. What will I tell the brothers at home about this place?* He looked beyond the open gates of the cemetery at the traffic winding around the street in front. Women carrying stuff on their heads. *Somebody oughta give these sisters a break.* Hot splashes of color flashed beyond the gates, the hubbub of people talking reached his ears in isolated patches.

Yeah, what can I tell the brothers about this place?

He stood, brushed his pants off, and slowly made his way back to the dregs of the party.

* * * * *

"What the fuck is this?! We give you a party and you disappear! What the fuck is this?!" *Five o'clock, three more hours to go before I'm free of your sick shit.* Helene chatted with three women in a distant corner, trying to pretend she didn't hear Fred's voice.

"Had to go out, Fred, had to say good-bye to a couple of people."

"That ain't no fuckin' excuse! We give you a party and you disappear! What the fuck is this?!"

Bop recognized the signs. Fred was in high gear now and nothing would bring him down. He didn't need a target or encouragement. Bop turned away from him and went to his room.

"Where the fuck you goin'?!"

Helene spoke from across the room: "He's got to pack, Fred. Remember, he's leaving this evening."

"Who the fuck asked you anything?! Huh, I don't need you to tell me a fuckin' thing! You understand what I'm sayin'?! I don't need you to tell me shit!"

Bop sprawled across the bed on his back and stared up at the ceiling. Going back home to the madness.

Back to the madness. Yeahhh, that's what it is. Chester L. Simmons had run it down to him a number of times, in a series of lectures.

"America is a mad place, Bop, 'specially for a black person. Think about it; we've been the best Americans America ever had; we've been better Americans than the Native Americans even. But the place is so mad, so Euro-crazed, they've never wanted to give us our righteous credits. Thus making us into schizophrenic types who go off and fight America's wars, do most of the dirty work, pay taxes, and try not to fall between the cracks.

"It's hard to say why the place is mad, but it is. Maybe it's got something to do with that original strain of VD them funky chumps from Europe brought over here."

Bop went in and out of a nod, a little high from an afternoon of sipping and strolling, trying to fix his focus on what he had to do when he made it back.

Why not go into journalism? All you got to do is

*know how to spell pretty good. Yeah, why not? No
need to make a liar out of myself by telling Uncle David
and Aunt Lu I'm going back to school and then copping
out.*

6:30 P.M. Time to do a last-minute check. Ticket, passport, money. He laid fifty thousand cedis on the bedside
table. Fred, here's some beer money.

Fred was still ranting and raving at Helene; the other
guests had dropped out. "Now you gonna tell me that these
niggers over here is better than them niggers over there!
Bullshit!"

"That's not what I said, sweetheart."

"What the fuck did you say?!"

They both seemed startled by Bop's reappearance with
his trio of suitcases. "Hate to interrupt you guys but I think
it's time for me to hit the road."

Fred blinked and hit a sober note. He could do that whenever he wanted to, it seemed. "Yeahhh, guess we better
start pulling it together. Check your stuff in and everything."

"I was thinking that I could take a taxi."

"What? And pay somebody twenty thousand cedis?
Lemme finish this glass and we can go."

"Uhh, Fred, you're not driving, right?"

"Nawwww, I'm drunk and fucked up. Helene is driving."

Complex man, full of twists and turns. They placed his
bags in the boot of the car and fifteen minutes down the
road Fred was dead asleep. Helene lit a cigarette and drove
silently. They pulled into the airport parking lot a few minutes after seven. Fred was snoring.

"Uhhh, Helene, you want to wake Fred up? I'd like to
say good-bye to him."

"You can't wake him up now."

Yeahh, you're right, lady; he's gone for awhile. Porters

snatched his bags and raced through the terminal. Chasing the cedi.

"Will he be OK?"

Helene gave a dry little laugh, "You think someone is going to steal him?"

7:33 P.M. The efficient British Airways crew was ready and loading them on. Bop turned to Helene, undecided as to whether he should hug her and plant a fake kiss on her cheek or....

She reached her hand out for a handshake and spoke in a low, solemn voice, "He wasn't always like this. We used to have a lot of fun together." And joined a crowd filing out of the terminal.

"Good evening, sah, welcome aboard. You're in seat 24A, a window seat. Enjoy your flight.... Good evening, sah, welcome aboard...."

Well, we're back to this again. Bop took his seat and peered out at the Africans going back and forth on the group.

Bye y'all; see you next time.

Next time. *When will next time be? Will I have to go back to jail before there's a next time?* A cold sweat erupted under his armpits.

No, no more jail for the brother. Nothing you can do in there but rot. No more jail. The plane was taxiing for a take-off.

Bye, y'all; bye, Elena, with your fine ass. When my cheeks start caving in and I find out I'm dying, you'll be the first to know. Bye, Patience; don't work too hard. Bye, Dew Drop. Bye, Betty in the Shalizar. Bye, Osu....

The plane was thundering off the ground suddenly and, moments later, circling Accra for its flight north.

"I say, d'you have the time? My watch seems to be on the blink."

Bop looked at the pale-faced man with the freckles who was speaking to him across the aisle. He held his wrist up to study the face of the watch, Ghanaian style, and announced, "My watch must be on the blink too; it says midnight."